Emma slurped the la carefully set the massive

"You know somet

damn long." She accen

a tortilla chip at Donovan.

"You weren't seriously involved with that banker." He took a swig of his beer. When he set it down, beer spilled over the top.

"I could have been. Stephen and I had a lot in common."

"Yeah? Like what?"

"We both volunteered for the Save the Seas charity." She ticked one item on her finger.

"Hmm…" His eyes narrowed. "What else?"

Emma screwed her face up. She was having trouble organizing her thoughts, and this interrogation was making her think too hard. She blinked.

"He's attractive. He's my age." She counted off two more fingers. She extended another finger, then hesitated. "Oh, yes! He has a good job. That's four reasons."

He shook his head. "Those are superficial rationales at best. They don't establish long term compatibility. Anything else?"

"Uh, he was a good dancer." She made a "voila" motion with her hands.

"Right." He set his beer down precisely on the mat. "It's clear to me that you could never have been deeply committed to him."

# Sanctuary on Victoria Island

by

Karen Andover

*Victoria Island Series*

This is a work of fiction. Names, characters, places, and incidents are either the product of the author's imagination or are used fictitiously, and any resemblance to actual persons living or dead, business establishments, events, or locales, is entirely coincidental.

**Sanctuary on Victoria Island**

Cover Art by *Kim Mendoza*

The Wild Rose Press, Inc.
PO Box 708
Adams Basin, NY 14410-0708
Visit us at www.thewildrosepress.com

Publishing History
First Edition, 2023
Trade Paperback ISBN 978-1-5092-4770-7
Digital ISBN 978-1-5092-4771-4

*Victoria Island Series*
Published in the United States of America

## Dedication

For my husband, for his unending love and support. For my sister, for sharing her wisdom.
And for my mother, for fostering a love of reading.

# Chapter 1

Emma Rutledge glanced at the clock on the dash of her car. Her fingers drummed in a staccato rhythm on the steering wheel. *Damn it. I better get there before my client.* It was a matter of personal pride for her and for the reliability of her family company, Rutledge Properties. Reputation was everything in the small island community. She excelled at finding the perfect home for her clients, and they were delighted with her. Her shoulders drooped. Too bad her boyfriend wasn't so delighted. She quashed that thought.

The ranch house was new to market, and she suspected it would go quickly. Set on an acre of land, it backed up to the intracoastal separating mainland Florida from Victoria Island. Homes with access to the inland waterway, which ran from Massachusetts down the length of the Atlantic coast, sold for premium prices. This property had its own dock, which was an attraction to her client who loved to fish.

Emma's cell phone piped the ring tone for her sister-in-law. "Sweet Home Alabama." She huffed and accepted the call.

"Hi, Ava, what's up? I'm showing Ed Morganfield another house. This one ticks all his boxes." She sighed. "If it doesn't, I may have to mediate with his wife. I suspect that the real issue is Ed doesn't like any of the properties because he doesn't want the divorce." She took a deep breath. "Sorry. I said I only have a minute, then I dumped all this on you. What's up?"

"Hi, Emma." Ava paused. Her normal enthusiastic greeting was muted as she continued hesitantly. "Uh, I'm glad I caught you. I won't keep you long. I just wanted to give you a heads up."

The smile melted off her face. Her hands clenched the steering wheel. *Can't be good news. When it rains, it pours.* Two days ago, Emma had closed on a house sale and thought she would surprise her boyfriend with a bottle of wine and a home cooked meal. Using her key, she had let herself in to his apartment. The wine glasses on the coffee table, mussed hair, and clothes in disarray told her everything she needed to know. Stephen had introduced her to Sandy, one of his coworkers, at a party a few weeks earlier. Since then, Emma had been going over and over that meeting in her mind. Had there been any telltale signs? Was she totally obtuse? Ugh... Was she the last one to know? She flinched as she recalled the lack of drama. Squaring her shoulders, she had excused herself and left. When Stephen had called to apologize the next day, she had ended their relationship. Maybe that was what was wrong with her choice of boyfriends. Hell, not just with this one. With them all. No real emotional involvement. She blew out a breath. *I'll be thirty in a few months. I always thought my life would be arranged by now. Settled. With a family.*

"What's wrong, Ava? Is it about Stephen? I was going to tell you before the news got out, but it looks like it's already public knowledge. I'm sorry you heard it from someone else. But I'm really okay. I'm embarrassed to say my heart isn't broken. It's just a bit humiliating." She put on her turn signal, slowed, and turned right, toward the north end of the island. "We're over. Or maybe we were finished, but I've only just realized it."

"Oh. So you've broken up? I hadn't heard. I'm so very sorry, Emma. But I'm glad to hear that you're doing all right. I know it sounds like a cliché, but you are so much better off without him. If you need to talk, I'm here for you." She paused. "Actually, I wasn't calling about Stephen." Ava's voice gentled. "I just wanted to let you know Donovan is coming home to stay."

"Oh." Her heart slammed against her chest. She hadn't expected *that* news. Old feelings of rejection welled up inside her. She struggled to keep her composure. A girl had her pride.

"Jack is going to tell you." Ava's voice softened as she continued. "But I thought you might want to be prepared when you see him. I didn't want you to be blindsided by the news. He's leaving the military. Jack has offered him a job as a commercial project manager at Rutledge's. Donovan will be looking for a place to live, and Jack has agreed to show him some properties." Ava was silent for a moment. "I think Jack is hoping you've forgiven Donovan."

Emma grimaced. Clearly Jack had told Ava about her childhood obsession with Donovan. *No one appreciates the messenger. So true. I've gotten over him. Why can't everyone else move on too? Small town life.* She pulled her thoughts together.

Sitting up straighter, she forced her voice to sound stronger. It was an old trick she had learned in drama class in high school. *Funny what you learn that sticks with you.* "Thanks, Ava. It will be great for Jack to have Donovan around. I'm glad he's safely out of the military." *That was nonchalant. I hope.* "I've got to go. I've just arrived at the property I'm going to show. I'm sure we'll catch up later."

"All right, Emma. I'll look forward to it." Ava's voice was quiet. Emma stiffened. *Didn't fool her...*

Her phone clicked just as Emma ended the call. Another call coming in. She narrowed her eyes as she glanced at the screen. Ann-Marie. *Better get this over with too. Everyone only wants to help.* She blew out a large breath and hit the answer button.

"Hi, Ann-Marie, I'm just about to meet a client to show a home. Can I give you a call later?"

"Hi, hon. I'm just calling to catch up. I thought you might need to vent about that asshole Stephen. I'm always up for that. Another man-whore in a long line of them. But we can talk later." Ann-Marie finally stopped her slightly bitter diatribe to take in air, and Emma jumped in.

"Thanks, Ann-Marie. I promise that I'm fine. Stephen is history. I'm better off without him." Emma effortlessly echoed Ava's pronouncement. She didn't have to force her voice this time. Even as she spoke the words, she knew they were true. She and Ann-Marie had drowned a lot of sorrows together in the five years since Ann-Marie had moved to Victoria Island, sharing all their heartbreaks. Except Donovan. She had never shared that part of her past. It was too raw.

"Are you sure?" They had had more than a few drunken tirades about men over too many glasses of wine. Perhaps more than their fair share—of both wine and poor choices in men. If she were honest with herself, Donovan was the reason she dated losers. Consciously or unconsciously, she sought out men who were the opposite of Donovan. Men who fit that category had trouble keeping jobs and being faithful. *Almost like I didn't want to take the risk of getting close to anyone.* She firmly shut those thoughts down and focused on the conversation.

"Yes, I promise you. I'm late for my client appointment, but we should meet up later for drinks."

"Absolutely. Six at the Sea Shack?"

The corners of Emma's mouth curled up slightly. They had spent many enjoyable happy hours at the Sea Shack, a local hangout popular with young professionals. Ann-Marie's exuberance would be a great distraction. No doubt they would drink a little too much, but they would firmly excise Stephen out of her life.

"Sure, that sounds good. I'll see you then. I'm sorry, but I've got to go now." Emma hit the button on the steering column to turn off her phone and turned into the driveway of the ranch house. She parked her SUV next to her client Ed Morganfield's battered white pickup truck. He was early. She sat there for a moment. Deliberately forcing thoughts of Donovan to the back of her mind, Emma surveyed the house with critical eyes. Set back at the end of a long gravel driveway, bordered on both sides by tall trees and shrubs, the house sat in dappled shadow. *Might want to thin the trees out a little for more curb appeal and to allow more light on the house.* She fought back the start of a slightly hysterical laugh. She pressed her hands on her cheeks and inhaled deeply. *I'm worried about a damn house when my life is about to implode. What if Donovan's bringing a girlfriend? What do I do when he inevitably hooks up on the island? Or the unthinkable. When he marries? Oh my God, maybe he's already married. No, Jack would have told me that. Definitely.* Tears pricked at her eyes. *I've been crushing on him since I was sixteen.* She hit her hand against the steering wheel. *Damn it. It's been fifteen years. I need to get over him once and for all. I'm better than that. I am better than that. Damn it, I'm so much better than that.* Maybe repeating it would help her believe it. She took several deep breaths and squared her shoulders back. She glanced around, but Ed was not in sight. *Thank goodness.*

Emma winced as she glanced in the rearview mirror of her high-end SUV and blotted her eyes with a tissue. *Thank heavens for waterproof mascara.* Her bright blue eyes, the signature feature of the Rutledge family, were red. *Not much I can do about that.* Her hand trembled as she reapplied the pale pink lipstick. The color smudged outside her lip line. *Damn it to hell.* She rubbed away the mess and tossed the lipstick in her purse. She tucked a stray blonde curl behind her ear. *Time for a haircut. No. Maybe a change of hairstyle. Get dumped. A former flame comes back to town. Change your hairstyle. Such a cliché. But it works. So who cares what anyone thinks?*

She smoothed out the wrinkles in her dress, a stylish multicolored sheath from a well-known designer. Wedge sandals made of a natural material that matched her large straw bag had her satisfied that she was put together, or at least not obviously distressed. She grabbed her handbag and keys and got out.

Pine needles crunched underfoot as she walked to the house. The tall spindly pine trees provided streaks of shade. A strong smell permeated the air. "Fox urine" she thought as she stumbled and reached out to steady herself on the porch fence. *Note to self. Pine needles are hell on sandals. I need to keep a spare set of more sensible shoes in my car for these outlying properties.* The lockbox with the key to the house was not fastened to the door. *How careless.* Maybe Pete had already opened up. She tried the knob. It turned easily, and she pushed the door open.

"Hello? Ed? Are you in here?" Her voice echoed in the vaulted entryway. The house was eerily silent. *Maybe Ed is down at the dock. That gives me a minute to look around.* Tall Grecian pillars framed the entryway. An elegant metal staircase with intricate scrolled posts split into double flights of stairs leading to a gallery overlooking the entryway. A large black metal chandelier trimmed with gold fittings cast a warm glow and reflected off the pale blue ceiling. *Huh. Pete Magnuson isn't doing his client any favors. I don't know why he said the property wasn't well kept and not ready for showing.*

She moved farther into the house, turning on lights in each room so the house would look its best. Her steps resounded on the tile floor. The late afternoon sun shone in through skylights in the ceiling as she entered the kitchen. White speckles in the black granite countertops sparkled and matched the kitchen cabinets. She trailed her finger over the granite surface, enjoying the cool feel of the stone. The kitchen windows overlooked the intracoastal waterway. *Wow. This kitchen alone will probably sell the house. If the rest of the house shows as well, the house will be off the market in no time. He's probably tucking this property*

7

*away for a client of his own. If he discourages viewings, the owner is likely to lower the price, which would be advantageous to his buyer. And he gets both sides of the deal.*

She passed through the kitchen into the living room. Sunlight streamed in through the patio doors. Beyond the paved patio, a grassy embankment transitioned to a reed bed bordering the river. A tall egret waded through the marsh searching for its next meal. *What an amazing view.* She opened the patio door, and the warm breeze collided with a stream of cold air from the house. She shut the door and turned to explore more of the downstairs.

The half bath was next in her exploration. The gleaming marble countertop set off a glass vessel sink. *This is move in ready. Ed wouldn't need to do any renovations.*

The cut glass crystal pendants shimmered and reflected on the oblong dining table as she turned on the chandelier light in the dining room. *If Ed buys this house, I'll buy that chandelier from him. Add a little class to my condo.* As she wandered through the dining room, she pulled her phone out of her purse to check for any messages from Ed. No signal. *That's the first downside to this house. I'll just take a quick look upstairs.* She ran up the stairs and opened the door to the owner's suite, flipping on the light. An enormous four-poster bed was the focal point in the center of the room. A chaise lounge added a touch of romantic glamour while a Juliet balcony gave a grand view of the intracoastal waterway. Excitement rushed through her. *This would appeal to a lot of couples. Even if Ed doesn't like it, I could sell this house in a minute.* She flipped open her notebook to review Ed's list of "must haves" in his home. Deep water access. No near neighbors. A short drive to his office. Under his maximum price. Her pulse quickened. *I can't wait to see his reaction.*

The attached bathroom door was closed. She eagerly pushed the door open, excited to see if the bathroom was as luxuriously appointed as the rest of the house. A rancid smell assaulted her. *Ugh!* Emma put her hand over her nose and ran her hand around on the inside wall, searching for the light. Just as she flicked the switch, someone grabbed her from behind. She gasped as the arm around her throat cut off the flow of oxygen. Her heart thudded in her chest as she clawed frantically to loosen the hold. The bathroom mirror reflected her assailant. His lank, straggly brown hair surrounded a bald crown, and a slightly bulbous nose was out of sync with his rail thin face and body. He sneered, exposing crooked yellow teeth. A faded T-shirt advertised a local radio station, and his holey jeans sagged around his waist.

"Don't look at me," he screamed, his dilated pupils giving him a crazed look. Emma hyperventilated as she struggled to get air. She twisted her body to try to release some of the pressure on her neck.

"Stop it, bitch." He jerked her head back, knocking her teeth together. "Don't fight me, or I'll hurt you real bad." He dragged her toward the bed. Panic rose up in her body. The man's body odor was overpowering, and she gagged as she inhaled. *I can't die this way. I haven't done everything I want to do.* "He-Help!" She slumped, throwing all her weight against him.

They fell back onto the bed, and he landed on top.

She recoiled from the stench of his foul-smelling breath. *Maybe Ed isn't here. Maybe that's not his truck. Does anyone know I'm here?* She fought a rising hysteria. *Will they find my body?* She reached up to push him off and slammed her head into his chin. He reared back from the blow. While he was momentarily distracted, Emma scrambled off the bed, but he grabbed her around the throat once again. Emma tugged at his arm, and he increased the pressure even more. Her vision went dark as if a shutter came down. She elbowed her assailant in the gut. "I'll kill you!" he snarled.

Emma didn't see how it could get worse. *Who will tell my family? Oh my God, I don't want them to have to identify my body. It can't end this way.*

"Stop struggling, bitch. I won't warn you again." His tone was vicious as he knocked her against the wall. A blinding pain in the side of her head where it connected caused the room to go fuzzy for a minute. Time slowed as thoughts rumbled through her mind. *I've got to do something. Jack always said fight with what you have. Anything can be a weapon.* She sank her teeth into the dirty flesh of her attacker's arm and gagged on the coppery taste of his blood in her mouth. He screamed and let her go. She spun around and he backhanded her across the cheek. Her head snapped back from the impact.

"What do you want?" At least his arm was no longer cutting off her oxygen. "I have money." She gasped. "Let me give it to you, and let me go. I won't say anything. I swear."

"Don't look at me." He backhanded her again, knocking her into the bedpost. Then everything went black and there was no more pain.

## Chapter 2

Something cool caressed Emma's face. The blackness slowly receded, and she faded in and out of consciousness. She groaned and opened her eyes. The room spun, and the back of her head throbbed. She reached up and her hand came away sticky with blood. *This must be the worst headache of my life.* She looked around. Where was she? Oh my God! She bolted upright as memories returned. A wave of nausea hit her. She struggled to keep the bile down.

"It's okay, Emma. You're fine." Ed's face creased with worry lines. He knelt next to her, wiping her forehead gently with a wet towel. "Just lean back. You fell and hurt yourself. I've called an ambulance. It should be here soon. Can you tell me what happened?" he asked as he sat awkwardly back on his heels.

"Um, I don't—I don't know." She moved her head, and queasiness assaulted her once again.

"Easy now." Supporting her back with one hand, he lowered her until she was lying down again on the carpet. "Stay still. I came into the house after inspecting the dock. I saw your car, so I started looking around for you. I found you in here on the floor. You hit your head and passed out. Don't move. You're still bleeding." He frowned at her with concern.

"No, no!" she rasped out.

Ed leaned down close to her face. "Hey, now, take

it easy. You've had a shock." He smoothed the hair away from her cheek.

"No, you don't understand." She tugged on his sleeve. "Someone attacked me. He tried to strangle me." *Why couldn't she make him understand?* "He could be here. We need to get help." Her eyes darted around the room. "We've got to get out of here. Don't you get it? He could kill us."

Clearly uncomfortable, he picked up her hand and held it. "Emma, there was no one here. You may be a bit confused. I've heard that blows to the head can do that. Please rest." He tilted his head. A siren blared. The noise increased as the emergency vehicle got closer. "Listen. Do you hear the clamor? That must be the ambulance. I'm just going to run downstairs and get the paramedics. Just stay here. Don't move." Ed patted her gently on the arm.

"Don't leave me." She clung to him, refusing to let go.

"Don't worry. There's no one here. I'll only be gone a minute." He rested his hand on her shoulder. "But I'll be within shouting distance the whole time." He put the wet towel in her hand and carefully guided her hand to her head. "Here, hold this on your injury. Keep the pressure on to stop the bleeding. I'll be right back."

Ed lumbered to his feet and hurried out the door and down the stairs to let the paramedics in. He returned in a few minutes with the ambulance attendants close behind him, guiding a stretcher on wheels. They wore the blue uniform of the local fire department.

One medic's wiry red hair, tied in a ponytail, fell

over his shoulder as he loped into the room. He set his medical bag down and crouched beside her, nimbly avoiding the pool of blood that had soaked into the carpet. "Hello, ma'am. Can you tell me your name?"

Red spots danced wildly before her eyes. She blinked once slowly, then again. No, not spots. Freckles. "I'm not that much older than the three of you. Not old enough to be called ma'am."

He chuckled. "I can tell already that you're going to be fine." He shined a penlight at her pupils.

Emma winced at the light and put her hand up to shield her eyes. "Emma Rutledge."

He made a "V" with his fingers. "How many fingers do you see?"

"Just two."

"Good. Can you tell me where it hurts, Emma?" He applied pressure to her head wound while his partner lowered himself slowly to the ground on her other side and put a blood pressure cuff on her arm.

"My head and neck." She reached up to show him.

"I can see that. You've had quite a blow to the back of your head. You're also going to have a nasty bruise on your neck." He lifted her a fraction. "I'm just putting a temporary bandage on your head to stop the bleeding. They'll take it off to examine you. Hold still. We're going to put a cervical collar on you. It's just a precaution. We'll take you to the hospital to get checked out."

Ed's gaze bounced from Emma to the EMTs. "Emma said someone tried to strangle her, but there wasn't anyone here when I found her."

The gray haired paramedic's attention pivoted to Ed. "Did you call the police?"

Ed shook his head. "No, I just telephoned for an ambulance as she was unconscious. She's only been awake a very short time. I didn't know until she woke up that someone had tried to choke her."

"No worries. We'll call it in on the way to the hospital. The police can meet us there." He gestured to his partner to lower the stretcher. "On three. One. Two. Three." They lifted her onto the gurney.

Emma reached a hand out to Ed. "Can you call Jack?" Her voice trailed off.

Ed touched her arm reassuringly. "Yes, of course. Don't worry. I'll take care of it."

They wheeled Emma out of the room. Ed followed slowly behind. As they loaded Emma into the back of the ambulance, Ed dialed Rutledge Properties.

Chapter 3

Donovan Evans pulled into the passing lane and overtook the rusted car with New York license plates. University stickers littered the bumper, and luggage was piled high on the rear seat. He powered up the windows to shut out the blaring music. *The farther I am from that car the better. I didn't get out of the military just to be taken out by a reckless driver on the way to a party at the beach.*

He flexed his fingers, releasing the death grip he had had on the steering wheel for the past few hours. *It's good to be home.* He glanced at the clock on the truck's console. *Good. Time for a quick detour.* He turned toward the center north of the island. Memories bombarded him as he drove slowly down the main street of the quaint downtown area. The old world ice cream shop with diamond lattice windows that he used to go to with his grandparents after his parents died was still there. *Time moves on, but some things don't change.* A shadow flitted across his face. Not everything had stayed the same. His grandparents were gone now. Jack Rutledge's parents, who had treated him as family, had passed on as well.

He shook off the sad thoughts. *This is the start of the next chapter in my life.* He ran a hand through his short brown hair. It was just starting to grow out from his military buzz cut.

He scrolled through his contacts and hit the call button on the steering wheel of his truck while tapping his finger. The phone rang repeatedly. "Come on, come on, pick up, Jack." A computer voice interjected and directed him to leave a message. "Damn voicemail."

"Hey Jack, just wanted to let you know that I'm on the island. I'll check into the Beaches Hotel and give you a call. I'm looking forward to seeing everyone at lunch." He hit the cancel button and ended the call.

He flexed stiff hands and exhaled deeply. *What will Emma think about my return? Had it just been puppy love? Have time and distance killed her interest? No point speculating. I'll know soon enough.*

He turned right at the first set of traffic lights out of downtown and headed toward the Beaches Hotel on the arterial road. Large oak trees formed a shady canopy over the road. Great white herons perched high in the trees. Despite their size, the slender branches of the tree barely registered their arrival. In just under twenty minutes, he pulled his black extended cab truck into the lane leading up to the hotel entrance. White porticos sheltered the uniformed valets from the burning rays of the late morning sun.

He pulled his bag out from the back and tossed the keys to the attendant. "Any scratches or excess mileage, and I'll be coming for you."

The employee leaned casually against a pillar. He glanced at the exotic Italian sports car he had just parked then at Donovan's rig and smirked. "Whatever you say, sir."

*I guess that puts me in my place.*

As he walked into the dimly lit resort hotel, he pushed his sunglasses to the top of his head. A blast of arctic air slammed him in the face. Like a dedicated bachelor avoiding bridesmaids at a wedding, he skirted around a group of tourists that gawked at a large driftwood sculpture that hung from the ceiling, and approached the front desk. The receptionist's heavily mascaraed eyes widened as she took in his leanly muscled and broad-shouldered frame. Her gaze drifted up to his face, taking in his military haircut and flashing with approval.

"Welcome to the Beaches Hotel."

"Thanks. I have a reservation."

After pulling out his wallet, he handed her his credit card. Her fingers flew over the keyboard pulling up his booking. She swiped his card.

"I hope you enjoy your stay, Mr. Evans." She circled his room number on the envelope and inserted the card key. "You're on the fifth floor. The elevators are around the corner." She gestured to the right. With a coquettish smile, she placed a business card in the envelope. "I'm Isabel, the front desk manager. If there is *anything* I can do for you to make your stay more enjoyable, please don't hesitate to let me know." She winked as she held the envelope out to him.

The less than subtle invitation in her gaze was met with outright indifference. "Thank you, Isabel." He took the packet from her and headed toward the elevator. The back of his neck tingled. He didn't look back, but he was pretty sure she would be still looking in his direction. In another place, or another time, he might have seen where her invitation would lead. But not now. His cell phone rang, and he pulled it out of his pocket. Jack's name appeared on the screen, and he hit the answer button.

"Hey, man, that was good timing. I just checked into my hotel." Donovan pressed the up button to call the elevator.

"Good," Jack Rutledge responded. "We've been looking forward to your arrival. We need to celebrate you rejoining the civilian world." He paused. "Listen, Donovan, there is a slight change in plans. Something's come up, and I've had to rearrange my schedule today. So I'll have to cancel lunch today. I'll explain when I see you tomorrow. I've got a meeting at one p.m., but it shouldn't take too long. I'll still be able to take you to show you the property afterward."

Donovan's lips pressed in a straight line. *So much for the "welcome home" lunch with Jack, Ava, and Emma.* His shoulders drooped before he hitched them up again. He could afford to be patient. There would be plenty of opportunities to see Emma. After all, he was home for good now.

"Sure, that would be great. I want to run some of my options past you."

"Have you had any further thoughts on the project manager job? Our commercial construction division is busier than ever. I'd love to have you on board."

"I'm still mulling it over." He paused. "After fifteen years as a Navy JAG attorney, it's been hard to give up the Navy, and now, practicing law? I appreciate the offer, but I have to admit I'm on the fence. I'm also considering opening a law practice, but I don't want to be another scavenger picking over the same bones as every other attorney on the island."

Jack laughed. "Well, my offer will stay open. Take your time thinking about it."

"Thanks. I will. Where do you want to meet? The

19

house viewing is scheduled for three p.m."

"Come by the house around two thirty. I should be free by then."

"Sure. I'll see you then."

"Bye."

*Good to know marriage hasn't changed Jack too much. Still no time for social niceties. I guess we have that in common.* The tension drained from his shoulders and his chest eased. It was good to be home. It was time to set his plans for the future in motion.

# Chapter 4

"Hey Jack, great to see you." Donovan grasped Jack's hand and slapped him on the back. He contemplated Jack's bloodshot eyes and stubble. Lines were clearly etched around his mouth. "Ava must be working you hard though. You look done in."

Jack scrubbed his hand wearily over his face. "Ava's fine, thanks." His mouth tilted up on one side. "She's treating me well. In fact, she's the best thing that ever happened to me." He hesitated. "It's something else. We had a late night with Emma yesterday."

"Is she still in her party phase?" An icy chill shot through him. Maybe the timing still wasn't right. There was a good chance it might never be right. *Damn.* His carefully thought-out plan was imploding.

Jack shook his head. "No, it was nothing like that. She was showing a house yesterday and was attacked."

"What? Attacked? Is she all right?" Vivid images of Emma covered in blood ran through his mind. *Emma just has to be all right. She has to be. I've waited so long to make my move. Have I waited too long?*

Jack released a long pent up breath. "She has a concussion and some bad bruising on her eye and neck. Some bastard tried to strangle her and then hit her on the head."

"What. The. Fuck. Did they catch the son of a bitch?" His nostrils flared, and he forced himself to

21

unclench his fists.

"No, not yet." Jack grimaced. "He knocked her out and fled. Her client found her and called an ambulance. But by that time her attacker was long gone. I spoke with the Acting Chief of Police, Deputy Chief Rawlings, at the hospital. Emma saw his face and gave the police a good description. Unfortunately, Rawlings doesn't inspire confidence. He's not holding out much hope that they'll find him. The Chief of Police, Ken Davidson, is away at training, but I've been in touch with him to see what he can do. Maybe he can put some pressure on Rawlings. I'm just not convinced that Rawlings is motivated to do any investigation. They fingerprinted the house, but it's for sale, so you can imagine the large number of people who have been in the house and touched things. They'll check all the usual haunts for the down and out." He paused. "Emma said the guy looked pretty rough. He might be homeless."

"Damn." Rage coursed through his body. "How awful for Emma."

"Yeah, that is pretty much how we feel. Anyway, Emma was kept in the hospital overnight for observation. Ava and I brought her to stay with us for a few days while she recovers. We didn't want her to be alone. We were up with her all night. She was pretty restless. She's bruised and shaken up. Ava and a friend are with her right now."

"Is she up for visitors?" Donovan exhaled noisily. "Can I see her?"

"Maybe another day." Jack put his hand on Donovan's shoulder and steered him toward the garage. "She's still pretty upset. Hell, we all are. I just keep thinking about what could have happened." He choked up.

Donovan glanced up the stairs before turning back to Jack. "She'll be okay. Emma's tough. And we'll all be here for her."

Jack nodded. "As soon as she's ready for more visitors, I'll let you know. I'm sure she would love to see you. Come on. Let's head out to the condo I wanted to show you. It will do us both good to get our minds off this situation. Emma is in good hands. Ava and Elsa, my housekeeper, are making sure someone is always with her. It seems to help Emma. She had a lot of nightmares last night."

Donovan glanced again toward the stairs leading to the second floor before looking away. Still lousy timing. A vise-like pressure squeezed his chest making it hard to get air.

A door creaked. Flip flops slapped on the stairs, and a dog's paws scrabbled on the hardwood floor. A voluptuous woman sauntered toward them. She wore jean shorts which were a tad too short and a bright pink tank top emblazoned with glittery letters *Salon by the Sea*. Her ample breasts spilled over the top. Long blonde hair, elaborately braided in an intricate fishtail style, fell down her back. A large, black dog hurled down the steps behind her, his tongue lolling out the side of his mouth.

Hands on her hips, she simpered as she approached them. "Hello Jack. Hello, fine thing."

Jack smirked. Heat rose up Donovan's face.

"Ann-Marie, this is Donovan Evans, a friend of the family. Donovan, Ann-Marie is a good friend of Emma's. And you remember Zeus, of course." Jack gestured to the dog whose tail twitched like a metronome. When the black Labrador nudged Donovan's hand, he reached down to scratch him behind the ears. Zeus' body wriggled with happiness.

Donovan held out his other hand. "How do you do?"

Ann-Marie raised an artificially darkened eyebrow and pulled him in to kiss his cheek. "Well, hello, sugar. That's how we say hello in the south." Her gaze traveled up and down him. "Any friend of the Rutledges is a friend of mine."

Donovan accepted the kiss but pulled back as soon as was polite. "It's always nice to meet a friend of Emma's." He searched for an innocuous conversation topic before settling on a time worn classic. "You're not from the island?"

Boisterous laughter caused her breasts to shake. "Now, sugar, what on earth gave it away? I'm from a small town in south Georgia."

"That would have been my guess." His mouth tilted up at the corners for a second before flattening. "How is Emma doing?"

"She's been sleeping fitfully. Bless her heart. Ava, Elsa, and I have been keeping her company. Poor thing is resting now, so I thought I would go back to the salon."

Jack nodded. "We're thankful that you've been able to spend some time with Emma today."

"My pleasure, Jack. I'll be back tomorrow to see her." She glanced over her shoulder and winked as she headed out the front door.

Jack looked at Donovan. "Ann-Marie can be a bit much. But you better get used to her. She and Emma are very close. You're going to need to win over Ann-Marie too if you want to get Emma."

*Guess I won't need to have that talk with Jack after all.* "As long as she is good to and for Emma. And she seems friendly enough, although I don't see what they have in common." He spread his hands palms up. "There must be more to her than meets the eye if Emma likes her."

Jack snorted back a laugh. "Be careful with that one. She can be a bit too friendly. Ava hasn't warmed to her. We better get started. We've only got a thirty-minute time slot to view the condo." Jack handed several printed pages to him. Donovan glanced at the top sheet which detailed the amenities in the ocean front condo. The men headed out to the garage.

Chapter 5

"Turn here." Jack pointed to an entrance to townhouse-style condominiums about fifteen minutes down the road. Turning in, he parked under the shade of a large magnolia tree. A jumble of sweet-smelling Asian jasmine ground cover tickled his nose and he sneezed.

"I bet you didn't have that problem at your desert posting."

"No. I'd forgotten how miserable I could get when it bloomed."

Jack removed the key from the lockbox and opened the door, leading into the bright and spacious open plan living room and kitchen.

Donovan cast an eye around the space. "It's move in ready."

"Come on and check out this view." Jack led the way to the French doors that opened onto a patio overlooking the ocean and flung them open. "This is what makes this condo special."

They stepped out onto the deck. In the distance, a shrimp boat bobbed in the azure waves as expectant seagulls circled above hoping for a handout. Vibrantly colored cabanas dotted the sand providing cover for sunbathers.

"Now that view makes putting up with allergies worthwhile." Donovan gestured to the patio. "I can just imagine throwing a party out here."

"Yes, definitely." Jack paused. "You probably know, but I should remind you. There are pluses and minuses for being right on the ocean. The sea air is hard on air conditioners and paint, so the condo fees are a bit higher. However, property on the oceanfront retains its value and desirability. This condo association permits short term rentals. So if you wanted to rent the property in your absence, or if you bought a family home, you could do so. And of course, you have the ocean front adding both enjoyment and amenity value."

"I appreciate the reminder about the ocean salt corrosion. One of the practical realities of living here." Donovan clasped his hands behind his back. "I've factored that ongoing maintenance into my budget."

The undulating waves crashed against the shore in a hypnotic rhythm. His mind wandered as he imagined Emma and himself sipping wine and enjoying the cool ocean breeze after a long hot day. *My life has been on hold for so long. It's time to start living the life I've always wanted.* Now that he had put his plan in action, it would be better to find out quickly if Emma wanted a relationship. Rip the bandage off fast.

"The owner's suite is this way." Jack's comment pulled him out of his thoughts. He directed him down the hall. "There is a half bath off the hallway, and then both bedrooms have attached bathrooms."

"I like that it's a good size and has a door out to the patio."

Jack opened the door to the attached bathroom. Behind a glass partition, a large soaking tub shared space with the shower, creating a wet room. An intricate pattern of various brightly colored mosaic tiles covered the floor. Dual sinks sat on a vanity covered by white marble.

"Whoever remodeled this did a great job. But I still want to see those condos we have appointments to view tomorrow."

"Works for me. It's always a good idea to see a number of properties for comparison, and in case you see something you like better. You should never buy the first place you see." He cleared his throat. "Now we've got the business over with. We've been friends for a long time. We've always been straight with each other."

"What are you getting at Jack? It's not like you to beat around the bush."

"Yeah, well, it's my sister we're talking about."

"Ah." Donovan slanted a glance at Jack. "Are you trying to ask what my intentions are?"

Jack was quiet for a moment. "I guess I am."

"I'll put all my cards on the table. I'd like to ask Emma out. If she'll have me. But if it sets your mind at ease, I'm hoping to have a future with her."

Jack inclined his head. "That's what I thought. Let's head back to the house. I'll start the barbecue, and we can catch up. Maybe Emma will feel up to joining us for dinner."

Chapter 6

The intoxicating aroma of lemons from a bowl on the oversize white marble island wafted through the kitchen. A dozen yellow tulips made a cheerful centerpiece and bar stools formed a crescent in the center of the room. A caterer's refrigerator hummed quietly in the background. Blue cabinets contrasted against the white stone floor.

Jack leaned down to kiss Ava.

"Hey, be careful. I've got a sharp knife." She cut the large yellow pepper and handed it to Emma, who brushed the vegetable with marinade.

Emma's appearance punched Donovan in the gut. Her complexion was as dull and pasty as the gray T-shirt and shorts that she wore. A cervical collar propped up her neck. Livid black and blue ringed her right eye, and limp blonde curls were plastered to her head.

Ava's face lit up. "Donovan, it's lovely to see you." He leaned down to give her a kiss on the cheek and a hug.

"You look beautiful as always, Ava." Her glossy brown hair was secured in an elegant chignon. A red and white Hawaiian floral sundress accented her slender figure. "It's good to see you again too. Thank you for inviting me for dinner."

Ava dismissed his thanks with a wave of her hands. "You know you're family, Donovan. You always have an open invitation. In fact, you're very welcome to stay with us. But if you'll excuse me, I better get moving or we'll be ordering takeout tonight." She looked over at her husband meaningfully. "Jack, will you help me fire up the grill?" Without waiting for his response, she took his hand and hustled him from the kitchen and out to the patio.

Emma methodically chopped vegetables, not making eye contact with Donovan. Zeus snored gently, a large black spot on the kitchen floor. An occasional yip disturbed his slumber as he chased rabbits in his dreams. Donovan moved across the kitchen to stand opposite Emma.

"It's good to see you, Emma. Jack told me what happened. How are you feeling?"

Emma looked up after a minute. "I'm fine, thanks." She returned her focus to the produce. "It's good to have you back. How long are you staying?" She pushed the sliced peppers around on the cutting board with her knife.

He wiped his sweaty palms on his pants and cleared his throat. "I'm here to stay. I've retired from the military. I'm considering what to do with the rest of my life. I have a couple of possibilities." He paused and waited, shifting on his feet, then continued after she failed to respond. "I'm thinking about opening a law practice. Jack has also offered me a job working with him as a project manager. I've got options."

Emma gazed determinedly down at her hands. After an uncomfortably long silence, she looked at him. "Oh. I wasn't sure if you were coming back to the island for good, or if you just wanted a vacation home."

"No, I'm definitely here to stay." Donovan sat

down opposite her. He cleared his throat. "I was hoping maybe you and I could have dinner? Catch up on all the news. Maybe when you are feeling better?"

Emma was quiet for a minute. Acid churned in his stomach. They weren't on the same page. He hadn't gotten this right. *Damn it to hell.*

Emma focused on cutting a carrot into equal size pieces. She finally answered. "I'm not sure I'm up for going out."

Donovan reached out to touch her but thought better of it and let his hand drop. "It doesn't have to be right away. It can wait until you're well again."

Emma looked up at him briefly, then returned her attention to the vegetables on the chopping board. "I just—" She broke off, swallowing deeply. "I just don't know that it would be a good idea." She set the knife down and combined the vegetables and marinade in the bowl, which added a liquid sheen to the contents.

Donovan let out a breath he hadn't even realized he was holding. He hadn't felt this awkward since he appeared to represent his first client at a court martial and the judge called him on the carpet for not being properly prepared. He looked at her resignedly.

"Maybe we can talk again in a few days?" he quietly asked. He swallowed the sudden lump in his throat. He wasn't going to give up. Nothing worthwhile ever came easily.

Emma nodded listlessly. The patio door slammed closed, and they both jumped. Jack and Ava walked back into the kitchen. Ava looked at them expectantly. Tension filled the room. Her face fell, and she sighed quietly.

"Emma, how are those vegetables coming? Ready

to make the kebobs?" Ava asked.

"Yes, all done. I'll just get the skewers." Emma used both hands to push herself off the stool. She crossed the kitchen and opened one of the kitchen drawers, rummaging around for the skewers. She frowned, and her movements became more frenzied. She slammed the drawer and jerked the one next to it open. Ava walked over and put her hand gently over Emma's.

"Why don't you go sit down in the living room and keep Donovan company? I can prepare the kebobs, and Jack can put the steaks on the grill."

"Sure." Emma's features remained flat.

Ava glanced pointedly at Donovan. At her look, he gently took Emma's arm.

"Come on, Emma. Too many cooks will spoil the barbecue. Ava wants us out of her kitchen." He took her hand and led her back into the living room where he sat down on the white upholstered sectional sofa and pulled her down next to him. She slumped back against the overstuffed throw pillows.

"How are you? How are you really, Emma?" He opened his mouth as if to say more, then stopped.

She touched the bruise on her throat. "I've been better."

His voice gentled. She glanced nervously around the room. "Do you want to talk about what happened at the house?"

"No. No, I don't!" A lump formed in her throat. "I'm sorry. I told the police everything already." She rubbed up and down her arms. "I don't want to revisit it."

"I find it helps to talk about traumatic things

instead of bottling them up. But of course, you have to be ready. There's no forcing the issue. How about a completely different subject?"

One corner of her mouth tilted up. "That might be best."

"I'd love your opinion on the property Jack showed me. It's a condo on the beachfront."

Emma hesitated. "I don't know, Donovan." She stared down at her hands. "That's kind of a personal decision. It either feels right to you or it doesn't. I'm not sure how I could help."

"I'd still value your viewpoint. We could go tomorrow after lunch?"

Emma twisted her hands, and her face lost some of the little color that she had. "I don't know, Donovan."

Ava came in search of them. "Dinner, folks. Everything is out on the patio."

Donovan leaned into Emma. "We can talk about this later."

Emma bit her lip and nodded weakly in response.

Donovan offered Emma his hand and pulled her to her feet. He opened the door to the elaborate patio. A long patio table was set up next to the infinity pool which overlooked the sand dunes, and the Atlantic Ocean. Donovan pulled out one of the wicker chairs for Emma and took a seat next to her. Jack set a platter of steaks on the table. Ava added the vegetable kabobs and baked potatoes.

After everyone was seated at the table, Jack opened a bottle of red wine, and filled their glasses. Jack focused on Emma. "Donovan is thinking about joining Rutledge Properties as our Commercial Project Manager."

"Yes, so he said. It will be nice for you to work together." Emma responded without looking up as she passed the tricolor pasta with olives and tomatoes to Ava.

Ava cast a worried glance at Jack. Uneasy with Emma's reaction, Jack tried another subject. "I'm scheduled to show Donovan two condos tomorrow, but Jeff Galbraith called today and requested a meeting on the county project. He's put up some roadblocks. If you're feeling all right, would you be able to show Donovan the condos? Of course, if you're not up to it, I'll put Jeff off. You're more important than any deal."

Emma sighed inwardly. She forced a smile. "It's all right, Jack. You've been trying to put that proposal together for a long time. I know it would be a real problem for you to reschedule Jeff. I'm sure I'll feel a whole lot better after another night's sleep."

"Thanks Emma. I appreciate it. I would like to finalize the contract once and for all."

"I appreciate it, too." Donovan slanted her a glance. "But only if you're feeling up to it."

Emma shifted in her seat and nodded.

Jack glanced at Donovan, raising his hands palms up as if to say, "I tried."

Ava's cell phone rang and she glanced at the screen. "I better take this. It's my brother. Excuse me. I'll just be a minute." Ava got up from the table and silently moved into the house.

Jack rubbed his chin as he watched Emma push food around on her plate. "Do you need to take more pain medication?"

"No, I don't think I'll take any more until bedtime. It makes me groggy."

"But if it helps the pain."

"I said I didn't want any more." She collapsed in on herself. "I'm sorry, Jack. I didn't mean to snap at you."

He put his hand on hers. "It's ok, sis." Jack glanced at his watch. "Will you excuse me for a minute? I'll just check on what's keeping Ava." He went into the house, closing the patio door behind him.

Jack found Ava in the kitchen. She turned and wiped away tears. He spun her back around and embraced her.

"Hey, love, what's the matter?" He tilted her head so she was looking up at him.

Pain etched deep grooves into her face. "That was Nate. My father's had a heart attack. He's in the hospital."

Jack rubbed her back soothingly and kissed her hair. "How is he? Let me call Nate."

"Nate said he's doing fine. The doctors think it was mild. I need to see him." Her voice trembled. "To make sure for myself that he's all right." She squeezed his arms.

Jack brushed a stray lock of hair off her heart-shaped face. "Of course, sweetheart. I understand. We'll drive up tonight so you can see your father first thing in the morning."

"Oh, thanks. That will be such a comfort to my mom too." Her eyebrows drew together. "But what about Emma?"

"Don't worry, sweetheart. I'll have a word with Donovan. I'm sure he'd be willing to stay with Emma. And Matt will be back in a few days."

"That should work. I don't want her to go home

where she would be alone overnight or even be here by herself. And Elsa will only be here during the day."

Wrapping his arms around her, he rested his chin on the top of her head. "One of the many reasons I love you. You're worry about Emma as much as your dad."

Ava retorted sharply. "Of course. Why wouldn't I? We're all family now."

Jack kissed her on the brow. "Go on and pack. I'll sort out Emma and Donovan."

"All right, thanks." Ava hurried out of the room.

Jack massaged the back of his neck. *How to finesse this with Emma?* As he opened the door, the ocean breeze rustled the rattan blinds. Emma turned and winced as she moved her neck. She stopped and angled her entire body toward him.

"Is everything all right? Where's Ava?"

Leaning down, he gave her a gentle hug. "I'm afraid her father had a heart attack. They don't think it's serious, but Ava wants to go up to Atlanta to see him."

Emma immediately nodded. "Of course. Please tell Ava's family I'll be thinking about them and that I wish her father a speedy recovery."

"Donovan, I know this hasn't really been the homecoming you were expecting. But I don't want to leave Emma here alone. And Zeus needs looking after." He reached down and ruffled Zeus' fur. "Will you stay here while we're gone?"

"That's not necessary." Emma averted her gaze and straightened her silverware in a neat row. "There's no need to inconvenience Donovan. I'm sure Ann-Marie would come over. Not, of course, that I need anyone to stay. I'm fine. I'm completely fine." Her demeanor telegraphed the opposite of her words. "I'm dealing with this." She waved a dismissive hand at Jack. "I'm not a child." Her cheeks burned.

Jack's forehead furrowed. "I'd feel better if Donovan stayed here, Emma. And there is no need for him to have the cost of a hotel when we have plenty of room here."

"Of course, I'll stay here with Emma. I'm happy to keep her company." He glanced over at her. "You've been through a traumatic event. It affects people in different ways. No need to worry about anything, Jack." He concentrated on Emma as he answered Jack. An emotion flitted briefly over Emma's face, but he couldn't identify it.

"Thanks. I knew I could count on you. Will you excuse me? I'm just going to put an overnight bag together as well. We'll leave as soon as possible." Jack headed inside and closed the door behind him.

Emma raised her chin. "You really don't need to stay. I'll be fine. Zeus is here." She gave the dog a hug, and he swiped his tongue over her face. "Tomorrow Elsa will be here. There's nothing actually wrong with me." She pulled a face and pointed to her neck. "This cervical collar is just a precaution. I may not even need to wear it tomorrow. Jack can be a bit overprotective at times."

"Not only do I need to stay, I want to stay. It would be my honor and privilege to look after you."

Emma bit her lip. She wished he meant it. Oh, he would do everything in his power to protect her. But she wanted another vow. To care for her. She closed her eyes as memories of her high school graduation party assailed her. Donovan had come as he came to a lot of the Rutledge family parties. Bolstered by her newfound independence as an "adult," she had cornered Donovan and declared her love for him. Blinking rapidly, she recalled how he had told her she was still a child and needed to grow up. She had hated him more than anyone at that moment. Her gut twisted painfully. The humiliation was still real even after all these years.

She had thought she had put her childhood emotions behind her. But over the years it had been clear to her that she still suffered from her infatuation. On some level she compared all the men she dated to Donovan. None of them favorably.

Jack and Ava walked back out to the patio catching the last of Donovan's statement. Jack's voice jolted her back to the present. "Good. That's settled. Donovan will move in here until we get back. That way, Ava and I won't worry."

Emma stifled her objections. There was no moving Jack or Donovan now. It was all but a *fait accompli*. If she protested anymore, it would just raise more questions. And Ava would worry, which wouldn't be fair. Her problems paled in comparison to Ava's at the moment.

Emma hugged Ava tightly. "Give your dad my best. Let us know how he is as soon as you can."

"I will."

Emma pulled Jack in tight. "Drive safely. And don't worry about me. I'll be fine."

"I can rest easy since Donovan is here. So be nice, sis. And take good care of Zeus." Jack leaned down and rubbed the dog behind his ear. Giving the dog a stern look, he lectured him. "You need to be on your best behavior." Zeus barked once in response.

Standing up, he turned to Donovan. "Would you

give me a hand with the bags?"

"Of course." They picked up the suitcases and headed out to the garage.

Ava wrinkled her brow. "Will you be all right? You had a pretty rough night."

"Of course." Emma deliberately downplayed Ava's concern. "Bad dreams can't hurt me. And I'm sure I'll be much better tonight. It was probably just the pain medication. Hopefully I won't need as much tonight."

Ava smoothed Emma's hair back. "I'll call as soon as I have any information."

"I'll walk you out." Emma waved as Ava got in the car. Jack reversed out of the garage and hit the button to close it behind him. Donovan and Emma both stared ahead as the door came down.

Finally, when the silence stretched uncomfortably long, Donovan turned to Emma. "I have to go check out of the hotel. Why don't you come with me?"

Emma didn't particularly want to go, but Donovan would be difficult if she didn't. "Sure. Let me just grab the house keys. Maybe Zeus wants to ride along too."

"Of course." He whistled, and Zeus came running. A fabric animal dangled out of his mouth. The white rabbit had long ears, with teeth protruding from its mouth, and held a carrot in one hand. One of the legs was missing, indicating its well-loved status.

Donovan's eyes crinkled. "Is the bunny going too?"

Laughter bubbled up, and Emma shrugged. "He likes to take it with him when he goes for a car ride. As a puppy, he would get motion sick, so Jack started the habit to distract him. The toy rabbit helped. And Jack no longer had to clean up the vomit in his car. Everyone was happy with the result."

"Works for me." He tossed the keys in his hand. "Let's head out."

Chapter 7

Fatigue washed over her, and Emma steadied herself against the wall once they returned. Her eyelids fluttered.

"You need an early night." Donovan traced the purple shadow under her eye. "How about we go to bed?"

"That works for me. Let me get you settled in one of the guest rooms." She led the way upstairs and opened the door to the room across the hall from hers. A hand-painted mural filled one wall, depicting a large sea turtle swimming with other denizens along the ocean floor. A rattan side chair and ottoman filled one corner. A double bed, covered in a blue comforter, dominated the room. She gestured to the attached bathroom. "There are fresh towels for your use. If you have everything you need, I'll say goodnight." The pain in her temples intensified. *Ugh. I need a dark room.* But she had to get Donovan sorted before she could do that.

Donovan cleared his throat. "Uh, goodnight. I'll be here if you need anything or have a nightmare."

"I'll say goodnight then." She turned and opened the door to the other guestroom. Zeus padded in behind her and went straight to the corner of the room. He turned in a circle before flopping down in the middle of a circular bed with his name embroidered on it. Resting his head on his paws, he shut his eyes. Emma closed the door and leaned wearily against it. *What a mess.* Her head pounded. And now she had Donovan to deal with. She pushed herself away. She was too tired to deal with him tonight. At least some sleep might help her headache.

After changing into one of Jack's old college T-shirts, she broke a pain pill in half and downed it with a glass of water. Crawling into bed, she pulled the covers up and turned out the bedside light. She quickly drifted off to sleep.

A few hours later she jerked awake from a drug induced sleep. *Damn medication.* As she rubbed her eyes, the room slowly came into focus. Zeus barked and scratched to get out. She groaned. "Zeus, next time when I let you out before bed, I want you to promise me you'll pee." Zeus' ears flattened against his head and he continued to scrape at the bottom of the door. Throwing back the covers, she swung her legs out of bed. "All right. All right. You can go out for a minute." Donovan rapped loudly on her door.

"You okay?" he shouted.

She put a hand to her throbbing head. "Yes, I'm fine, but I think Zeus needs to go out." She struggled to hold on to the dog as he twisted his body. He stopped barking but began a high-pitched whine.

"No, he doesn't. Lock your door and stay inside until I return for you. I mean it, Emma!" He pounded on the door in emphasis.

*Well, he's pretty damn grumpy when woken up in the middle of the night.*

She flipped the bolt on the door. The easiest course of action was to follow instructions and argue later. She went into the bathroom and splashed water on her face, trying to clear the fuzziness. The pills helped her sleep, but the hangover from them was almost as bad as the pain from her injuries. She sighed. Not much of a choice.

"Come here, Zeus. I'll let you out in a few minutes." Zeus padded back to her, his body quivering. His nose pointed to the door.

## Chapter 8

Loud popping sounds had woken Donovan from a deep sleep. Rolling out of bed, he hit the ground. *Fuck. Gunfire. Downstairs. Emma.* He had jumped up and reached into the back of the nightstand where he had stashed his handgun. With goosebumps on his arms, he had rushed to check on Emma. *Thought my days of being under assault were over. Thank God Emma's okay.* He held his gun pointed down as he crept down the stairs. The shots had stopped. Crouching below window level, he scouted around the house. The front door and windows were riddled with bullets. Careful to stay to the side of the windows, he flipped on the outside lights. No one was visible in the yard. Keeping the inside lights off, he worked his way around the house. The rear door and windows were intact. He threw open the door to the garage, flipped on the light, and dove in. All clear.

After running back up the stairs, he knocked sharply, and she unlocked and opened the door. Struggling to hold the squirming dog, she wrapped both hands around his body.

"You can let him go now." At his words, she released Zeus and he scrambled to get traction on the hardwood floor as he ran out the door. He flew down the stairs, his claws clicking as he raced through the house.

Emma shuffled back a step at the sight of his gun. Her mouth went dry. "What's going on?" she whispered.

Setting his gun on her nightstand he motioned for her to sit on the bed and sat down next to her.

A jolt of electricity shot up her arm when he took her hand in his. He exhaled deeply. "There's no easy way to say this. Someone sprayed the front door and windows with bullets."

"What!" She flinched. A weight on her chest constricted her lungs. *Someone wants to kill us.* "Wait a minute. You knew that and went out there? You could have been killed!" Anger roiled up through her body and she skewered him with her gaze. "What on earth were you thinking?"

A slow fury consumed him. "I was thinking I'm armed and trained. I was thinking I needed to protect you. I needed to keep you safe." He released another breath and pulled her flush against his chest. Despite her anger, she clung to him, and he clasped her tight.

Emma shivered. "Sorry. I didn't mean to yell. I just don't want you to get hurt on my account." She sniffled.

He rocked her gently as if she were a child, and his anger evaporated.

"Hey now, there is no need to worry. I had a target on my back in the military for years. I'm not about to take a bullet now that I'm out. That's not in my life plan." He chuckled as he stroked her back gently and continued to sway.

After what seemed like a lifetime, but in reality was only a few minutes, he released her. Meeting her gaze, his expression grew somber. "I need to go call the police. Are you going to be okay?"

"Yes. Of course." She sat up straight. "I'm fine. Go ahead and make your call." Feelings of shame overwhelmed her. He had risked himself for her. And what had she done? Stayed safe behind a locked door.

"That's my girl." He touched the tip of her nose with his finger. "I'll be right back." Picking up his gun, he closed the bedroom door behind him. In his room, he put the gun back in the nightstand drawer. He dialed the police dispatcher.

"Shots fired. 15 Ocean Avenue. Can you send a patrol car?"

"All right, sir. Are you in immediate danger?"

"I think they're gone. But I can't be sure."

"I've dispatched help. Stay inside and wait for the officers."

Hanging up the phone, he pulled on a T-shirt and jeans. He slipped his feet into loafers, then ran downstairs and waited to the side of the windows for the police. The inside lights remained off so he wouldn't be a target in case whoever had shot out the windows came back. Lights were flicking on up and down the street. Sirens blared in the distance, growing louder.

Within five minutes, a black and white patrol car, lights flashing, pulled into the driveway. Donovan opened the door and raised his hands in the air. The cool night breeze stirred the large potted plants in the entryway. Miraculously the vegetation had survived the shooting.

A spotlight shone in his face. Squinting at the bright light, he shouted to the officers. "I'm Donovan Evans. I called in the gunfire."

"Hey, man, Donovan, is that you? It's Mike Jefferson. I heard that you had left the military and were returning to the island." One of the policemen raised his hand in greeting. He turned to his companion. "It's fine, Jerry. You can move the spotlight away from him. He's friendly." The other officer lowered the light, and Donovan moved forward.

"Hi, Mike. It's been a while since high school. It's good to see you, although I wish it wasn't under these circumstances."

"Good to have you back. I'm a detective these days, but we've got a lot of officers out sick, and I'm helping out with street patrol." Mike clasped his hand and thumped him on the back. He gestured to the other officer. "This is my partner, Jerry." Donovan turned to Jerry and shook his hand.

Jerry whistled. "What's going on? Looks like you've had some trouble." The front door and windows on either side were littered with bullet holes. The entryway light reflected off the broken glass littering the porch. Casings were strewn on the driveway.

"Some cowardly asshole did a drive-by and sprayed Jack's house with bullets. Come see for yourself." Donovan gestured to the front of the house.

"Anyone hurt?"

"No. It was only Emma and I in the house. We were asleep in the bedrooms."

"Glad you're all safe. Did you see what happened?" Jerry flipped open a notepad and took a pen out of his pocket.

"No. Unfortunately, the shots woke me up. By the time I got to the window, the car was already well down the road. So I can't give you a description of the car or driver."

"Pity." Mike raised an eyebrow. "Has Jack pissed off anyone lately?"

Donovan shook his head. "That's a good question, but the answer is not that I know of. He's in Atlanta tonight with his wife. I'll wait until tomorrow to tell him about this."

"All right. Jerry, can you call this in? We'll need the forensic unit out here."

"On it." Jerry returned to the patrol car to use the radio.

Mike narrowed his eyes. "I know Jack has security cameras on the house. We'll contact the company for the footage." He scowled. "Maybe we'll get lucky, and they'll have caught the car on tape. We'll take some pictures of the damage and file a report. This is Jack, so the police chief will want to be briefed first thing in the morning."

Donovan's eyebrows drew together, and Mike shot him a side glance. "Something you want to share? Any problems other than getting shot at?"

Scanning the damaged door and broken windows, Donovan ran a hand over the stubble on his jaw. "Any chance this is about Emma, and not Jack? She saw her assailant and can identify him. Someone trying to scare her off? They haven't caught the guy."

"It's possible." Mike lifted his shoulder in a half shrug. "I was sorry to hear about the assault. The island isn't the same as when we were growing up. We have all the big city problems now, if only on a smaller scale."

"Is there any update on that case?"

"It can't hurt if I bring you up to speed. We found

48

propane tanks, glass equipment, and plastic containers with attached hoses. Also, rubber gloves and respiratory masks. And a ton of chemicals. In short, everything you need to cook up some meth. It was all down in the boat house. Quite a sight." He glowered.

"Damn. You think the vacant property was being used as a meth lab and Emma stumbled upon one of the meth addicts? Or the cook?"

"That's the current working theory."

"Any progress on finding her attacker?"

"No." Mike shook his head. "We're working it hard though. You know that most crimes are solved quickly or not at all."

"That's what I'm afraid of."

"The chief sent a black and white around to the usual places. You know, where the homeless people set up shop. No luck yet, but we feel pretty confident we'll track him down. Emma gave a great description." He waved a hand at the shattered windows. "You need help boarding things up?"

"Thanks, but I've got it. Jack has metal hurricane shutters. I'm just going to lower them over the broken windows and door. It will cover the damage and provide security."

"Sounds like you have everything under control. I'll ask Dispatch to have a patrol car cruise the area tonight and over the next few days. Oh, and I'll see if I can't get some of your neighbors back to bed." He gestured across the street to the crowd gawking at them.

Jerry signed off the radio and slammed the car door. "Forensics will be here first thing in the morning. None of the onlookers saw anything helpful. That's all we can do for now." He flipped his notebook closed.

Mike nodded his thanks. "Since you finished checking if anyone saw anything, let's get the crowd disbursed."

Mike walked toward the neighbors gathered across the street. "Nothing to see folks. Go on home now."

Donovan headed to the garage where the operational controls for the state of the art motorized hurricane shutters were located. Flipping the switch, he lowered the shutters. The metal screens covered the front door and the glass panel windows to the right and left of the door.

When they were fully deployed, he went in search of Emma. He found her pacing anxiously in the living room. Zeus followed on her heels.

She stopped when he approached. "What did the police say?"

"Come on. Let's sit down, and I'll fill you in." As he steered her to the living room sofa, his gaze wandered down to her long legs which were barely covered by the T-shirt. Her cheeks flushed. Donovan grabbed a throw off the back of the sofa and wrapped it around her shoulders.

"Thanks." She pulled the throw more closely around her and sat down.

Donovan filled her in on what Mike had told him.

She whipped her head around and then winced at the pain. "A meth lab! Here? That's unbelievable. Nothing like that happens on Victoria Island."

Donovan shook his head. "Unfortunately, methamphetamine, like other illegal drugs, is everywhere. On the positive side, the police think there's a good chance they'll find the guy who assaulted you."

"Oh, good!" She slumped against the back of the sofa. "Would I have to testify?"

He stroked her arm gently. No point keeping the truth from her. She would learn it sooner or later. "You might have to identify the guy in a lineup, and yes, it is likely you would have to testify. You might get lucky and not have to if he pleads guilty. But hey, we're getting ahead of ourselves. You don't need to worry about that now. And I'll be with you throughout the whole process."

She let out a pent-up breath. "Do you think the shooting had anything to do with the meth lab and my assault?"

Donovan was silent for a minute, trying to decide how to respond. Emma needed to be fully informed. In measured tones, he replied. "It's entirely possible, maybe even probable. I don't see the shooting as random. I'll talk to Jack tomorrow, but I doubt he has angered anyone enough to take pot shots at him. So yeah, in my view it's likely that it's related to your assault. Maybe they want to scare you. If he knows you saw him…" He paused, and Emma nodded. "He might want to scare you from telling the police or cooperating any further." The color drained out of her face.

He put his arm around her shoulder. "Hey now. Take it easy. We're good tonight." His fingers massaged her shoulder in a soothing rhythm. "The police have stepped up patrols. They'll be doing regular drive-bys. The house alarm is on. Jack's security system is one of the best. The hurricane shutters are down, so we're safe. No one can get at us. Let's get some sleep. Things will look better in the morning."

She let him steer her up the stairs, stopping only to

call for Zeus who came running from the kitchen. Emma paused at her door.

"Donovan?" She chewed on her bottom lip.

He turned. She fiddled with the silver rope bracelet she always wore, twisting it around on her wrist. He put his hand gently on hers to stop the nervous habit. "Yes?"

"Stay with me tonight? I can't stop thinking about what happened." Her hand shook. "How we could have died." She stared at the floor. Her words were almost inaudible.

His expression softened. "Of course."

She climbed into bed. Zeus pawed at his bed to dig a more comfortable patch before settling down. Picking up the blanket from the bottom of her bed, Donovan went over to the chaise lounge near the window. He tugged his shirt over his head and unzipped and pulled off his jeans. Wearing just his boxers, he settled on the chair. She pulled the covers up to her chin as she watched him shift uncomfortably on the divan.

She bit her lip as he stretched out on his makeshift bed. His legs hung over the end by a foot. "You'll never sleep there." She held up the covers on the other side of the bed.

He raised an eyebrow. "You sure?"

"Of course. We're both adults."

He slipped under the covers. Reaching up, she turned out the light and rolled over with her back to Donovan.

He settled down for a long night, knowing that it would be impossible to sleep.

Chapter 9

The sun rose over the Atlantic Ocean, pierced through Emma's ocean-side bedroom window, and woke her from a deep slumber. A heavy arm draped around her waist, pinning her against a hard body. Donovan's crotch pressed tightly against her bottom. She kept her eyes shut, feigning sleep while she contemplated how to extract herself.

"Good morning. I know you're awake," Donovan murmured in her ear.

"Uh huh. I can feel you're up." She cringed at the tactless words. "I mean, yes, I'm awake too."

Donovan moved his arm, and she sat up, pulling the covers up to her chest. Donovan shifted and extricated his legs out from under the covers. He sat with his back to her.

Emma hugged her knees to her chest. "Thank you. For staying last night. For everything. Jack will be very grateful that you took care of me."

Donovan glanced back over his shoulder at her. "You're welcome." A pause. "I didn't do it for Jack."

"Huh?"

"I did it for you, Emma." Donovan gazed directly at her.

"For me? Oh, yes, I appreciate it. You've been a great friend to the Rutledges. To us all."

Donovan got up and picked up his pants from the

chair. Stepping into them, he zipped and buckled his belt. His movements snapped with irritation. She watched him in frozen fascination.

He grimaced. "I did it for you. It's always been about you." He spoke slowly and spaced each word out.

"Well, but…" Emma clasped her hands around her stomach.

"You were so cruel to me. You treated me like a silly child. At my party."

He pinched the bridge of his nose and sat down next to her. *It's time to put all my cards on the table.* "At first you were too young. I didn't mean to hurt you at your graduation party. I could have handled it better. As soon as I spoke, it was clear you took what I said the wrong way. I just meant that it wasn't our time yet. Whether you want to admit it or not, you still had some growing up to do." He pressed a finger to her lips to stop her protest. "There were still too many years and too much life experience between us. It wouldn't have worked. We were at different stages in our lives."

Something flickered in her eyes. "But later…."

Donovan exhaled loudly. "And then you were old enough, but I wasn't in a good place for you. Long distance relationships are difficult. And being in the military complicated things. I made a decision not to pursue you then. But I'm out now. And Jack told me you're not in a relationship. So what I want to know is how you feel about me. Whether you want to give 'us' a try. If you don't, I'll move on and never say another word." Donovan's gut churned while he waited for her response.

"Oh."

"Oh?" Her answer pierced his heart like a dagger.

"Not quite what I was hoping to hear."

"That's not my answer. I'm just processing." She studied him. "I carried a torch for you for the longest time."

He ran a hand through his short hair causing it to spike. "It was probably inevitable. A friend of your older brother's. Bird in hand and all that."

A rush of anger roared through her. "Don't you dare be so dismissive. It wasn't just some teenager's first passion for me. I grieved for you, but I finally moved on. Or so I thought." She gulped in air. "It's always been you for me, Donovan. That's why my relationships have never worked out. I compared everyone to you. And they couldn't compete with you. I've tried so hard to forget you. And now this." She gestured at the two of them together. "I just don't know."

Leaning over, he took her chin in his hand and tilted her face. He gently pressed his lips against hers in a tentative kiss. She forced herself to not respond. His hands encircled her waist and pulled her closer. He deepened the kiss, but she refused to part her lips. *Damn him. He doesn't just get to walk back into my life after fifteen years and get his way. Arrogant asshole. Thinking I should just fall into his arms.*

The cell phone on the nightstand warbled. He pulled away slowly, his breathing ragged. Picking up the phone, he handed it to her.

She blindly hit the answer button. "Uh, hello…"

"Good morning, Emma. It's Elsa. I'm here, outside." Elsa clipped her words. "Why on earth are the hurricane shutters down?"

"Oh. Hi Elsa. I'm sorry—it's a long story. I'll fill

you in over a cup of coffee. I'll be right down to let you in through the garage."

"See you in a minute."

"I'll be right there," Emma confirmed and hung up the phone.

"Jack's housekeeper is here." Twisting her bracelet nervously, she studiously avoided his gaze. "Maybe I should give her time off until this is sorted? I don't want her mixed up in this, whatever this is. I don't want anything to happen to her." As she contemplated what to do, Emma chewed her bottom lip.

"That's probably a good idea." She stood up to leave, but he reached out to grab her arm. "We're going to have to talk about this. You can't just walk away."

"Actually, I can." She pulled on a bathrobe and crisply tied the belt.

He sighed. "While you let Elsa in and update her, I'll give Jack a call." Donovan reached for his phone.

Yanking open the door, Emma ran downstairs to let Elsa in.

Chapter 10

Donovan punched in Jack's number. While he waited for Jack to pick up, he paced the room.

Jack answered after a few rings. "Hey, Donovan."

"Hi, Jack. How is Ava's father?"

"He's doing well, thanks. They're going to keep him in the hospital a couple of days, but the doctor thinks he'll make a full recovery. Ava and I are going to stay here for a while to support her mother. Can you stay longer with Emma?"

"Yes, of course. I'll take care of Emma. Which leads me to the reason I'm calling." Donovan broke off, searching for the right words.

"Yeah?" Curiosity rang in Jack's voice.

"I have some bad news." Donovan paused. "Late last night a gunman shot out your front door and windows. Emma and I, and Zeus, are all fine. We were upstairs."

"What the hell?" Donovan could hear Jack turning the air blue and Ava's questioning voice in the background. "We'll come back today."

"No, Jack." Donovan rubbed his temple "Listen to me. You and Ava need to stay in Atlanta. Take care of Ava's parents. You know I'll protect Emma with my life."

"I know." After a moment, Jack responded further. "I trust you."

"Good. Then let me do my job." He massaged the back of his neck. It had been a long night. "I'll be with her twenty-four/seven."

"Is she okay? It's been a tough few days for her."

"She's a fighter. And she's resilient. Getting to the bottom of what's going on here is my priority." Donovan sat on the side of the bed. "Let me fill you in on what Mike told me. I can't help but think it's related to the meth lab. Emma saw something that they want to scare her into forgetting. Unless of course you've pissed off someone? Screwed someone in a business deal? Anything personal?"

Jack was silent for a moment. "There is something I need to tell you. I had a problem with theft from the company a few months ago. But the police made arrests. The thieves are tucked away in jail pending trial. They haven't been able to make bail so they're out of the picture. So the bottom line is no. I don't know of anyone who would have a grudge against me. Or Rutledge Properties, for that matter. I negotiate hard, but I expect most people would say I'm fair."

"I had to ask."

"Is Emma on board with you protecting her? You saw how she acted when I suggested you move in. I don't need to tell you that she was reluctant to have you stay there. She's still a bit sensitive about you."

"Yes, she seems okay with me guarding her." *Mostly. I hope.*

"You know you're like a brother to me. Just keep me posted on everything. I'll text the maintenance crew we have on retainer to start the repairs."

"Thanks. I'll let Emma know. Don't worry, I'll send you regular updates. By the way, Emma's given

Elsa time off until we get this cleared up to keep her out of harm's way. This morning Emma and I are going to talk to the police chief to see what else we can find out."

"Good. We'll talk soon."

Chapter 11

The island's police station was located a few miles north. Donovan concentrated on the traffic and swerved to avoid a car with out of state plates that slowed and made a random U-turn, halting traffic in both directions. Donovan shot Emma a look, but she continued to stare out the side window. "Are you worried about the police chief? We'll be there in a few minutes, so if anything is bothering you, now is the time to talk about it."

"I'm not worried."

"All right, then." His hands tensed on the steering wheel as he focused on the traffic.

He turned into the parking lot of the sprawling government building, a single-story edifice taking up an entire block. Clumps of monkey grass grew together to form a green carpet, punctuated only by slender palm trees. A state flag flapped in the breeze. Police cruisers were parked two deep and locked behind a chain link fence in the back of the building.

Donovan pulled into a parking space and cut the engine. "Come on. Let's see what we can find out."

In the reception area, white plastic seats and gray walls lent the reception area a grim appearance. They approached the plump, middle-aged woman sitting at a desk behind a glass barrier. She took off her reading glasses and let them dangle on a chain around her neck.

"Good morning. Can I help you?"

"Can you tell the chief that Donovan Evans and Emma Rutledge would like to see him?" Donovan stood in a relaxed stance; his hands clasped behind his back. The receptionist ran a hand self-consciously through her graying hair. Emma resisted the urge to roll her eyes.

"Of course, sir. I'll let him know you're here." Picking up the phone, she dialed a three number extension. She spoke softly for a moment and then hung up. "Please have a seat. Acting Chief Rawlings will see you in a few minutes." She gestured toward the rows of chairs.

Within just a few minutes a man with salt and pepper hair and a pale complexion, highlighted by red blotches, opened the door to reception. His protruding belly threatened to pop one of the shirt buttons on his uniform. He hitched his belted uniform pants up as he sauntered towards them.

"Mr. Evans, Emma, I'm Acting Chief Rawlings. Come on back." His voice boomed across the lobby. "Mabel, honey, will you bring three coffees back for us?"

"I'll have them in a jiffy, Chief." Mabel had a spring in her step as she walked to the kitchen area.

They followed Chief Rawlings past a number of officers at desks. Fake potted plants acted as separators between the cubicles. The clatter of typing on computer keyboards and phones ringing reverberated in the cavernous room. A glass wall separated the chief's office from the bullpen. Ushering them inside, he closed the door and blocked the noise.

"I'm using Chief Davidson's office while he's

taking a three-month long course at Quantico. The chief is a big supporter of continuous learning." He shrugged. "I believe in doing the job, not sitting in a classroom. I'm his deputy, so I'm fully up to speed on how things are run here. Now, how can I help you folks?" He sat down behind the desk, legs spread wide. He clasped his hands together over his belly, the chair creaking as he leaned back. Stacks of file folders and loose paperwork cluttered his desk. Framed photographs of Rawlings with politicians and other local luminaries hung on the walls.

"It looks like you've made yourself right at home." Emma gestured to the pictures.

"The public need stability and continuity in leadership. When I meet with citizens, these photographs show them my experience." Rawlings cleared his throat. "It's reassuring to them."

"Chief Rawlings," Donovan leaned forward in his chair, "as you may know, a drive-by shooter shot up Jack Rutledge's house last night."

"My officers keep me informed of everything that happens on the island. Terrible. Just terrible." Rawlings shook his head in disgust. "Don't know what's happening to this island. Not the way it used to be." He tilted his head at the sound of tapping. "That must be Mabel."

Donovan jumped up and opened the door.

"Come on in, Mabel, honey." He waved his hand in a welcoming gesture. "Mabel here is the heart of the Victoria City police. I just don't know what we would do without her."

Mabel flushed. She handed the mugs to Emma, then Donovan, and finally the chief.

"Thank you," Emma murmured. Donovan nodded his thanks.

Donovan took a sip before setting the cup down. His lips pinched together. "What are you doing to investigate the shooting?"

"Well now, boy, unfortunately, you haven't given us much to go by. Not that I'm blaming you of course." Rawlings held his hands up as if to placate Donovan. "No, siree. Not many men would have had the presence of mind to be able to identify the car."

Donovan clenched his jaw. *What a patronizing ass.*

He kept his voice even. "Don't you think it's likely the shooting is related to the assault on Emma?"

Rawlings ran his hand over the top of his head, smoothing his well-oiled hair. "Now why would you think that? Is there anything you haven't told me? You're some sort of fancy navy lawyer, aren't you?"

"You don't have to be, as you say, a fancy navy lawyer to make the connection." Donovan balled his fist. "Isn't it obvious? There's no other motive. Jack confirmed to me that there is no one who would have a reason to hurt him."

"No need to get all riled up." Rawlings held his hands up in a calming gesture. "I've got my boys visiting the homeless camps. Don't you worry, Emma. We'll find the monster who did that to you."

Donovan muttered an oath.

Rawlings' eyes narrowed. "Did you say something?"

"Just clearing my throat." He rubbed the back of his neck. "All right. Thanks for your time, Chief. We'd appreciate being updated on any progress." Donovan stood up, and Emma followed suit. He held his hand up as the chief started to stand up. "We'll see ourselves out. Thanks for your time."

Weaving their way through the maze of cubicles they exited back to the lobby. Emma nodded to the cheerful receptionist. *Not her fault she works for an ass.* Emma didn't speak until they were outside the building.

"Why do I get the feeling the chief isn't working that hard on my assault or taking the drive-by shooting seriously?" Emma mused quietly.

"Yeah. I get that impression, too." Donovan's mouth twisted. "I thought Jack was friends with the chief of police. I'm not impressed that he chose Rawlings to fill in for him."

Emma's face softened. "Jack respects Ken Davidson. But smalltown politics being what they are, I'm not sure Ken had much choice in appointing his temporary replacement. I don't think Rawlings is bad or corrupt, just lazy and disinterested."

"Huh. I won't argue with that."

Chapter 12

Heat radiated from the large picture windows in Jack's living room. Donovan lowered the blinds to block the afternoon sun. Emma stroked Zeus as he lay curled up next to her on the sofa. When her cell phone rang, she glanced at the screen, her face tightening.

"It's Rawlings." She hit the answer button and put the call on speaker. "Hello."

"Emma, this is Chief Rawlings." His voice thundered over the speaker. "I've got good news for you, little lady. We've made an arrest in your assault case. Of course, it was only a matter of time. My boys are well trained and dedicated. They've done me proud."

Emma covered her mouth with a hand. "That's wonderful news, Chief." She sagged against the back of the couch. "I appreciate all the work your officers have done on my case."

"Not at all. Now, I'd like you to come in for a photo array. Oh, sorry, little lady. That's a lineup using photographs. We need to see if you can positively identify your assailant."

Emma rolled her eyes at the chief's patronizing explanation but kept her tone pleasant. "Of course, Chief. What time do you want me to come in?"

"I'll have an officer available for the lineup at three p.m. if you can make it then."

"Three it is. We'll be there." She disconnected the call.

Tapping her fingers lightly on her phone she eyed Donovan thoughtfully. "Hmm…what do you make of that?"

He rubbed the back of his neck. "I'm not sure. I'll give Mike a call and see if he can give me the real story."

"While you do that, I'll make us some lunch." Emma retreated to the kitchen.

Donovan pulled up his contacts on his phone and hit the button for Mike. "Hey, Mike. This is Donovan. The chief just reported that an arrest was made in Emma's assault case, but he was a little short on details. Anything you can share?"

"Yeah. Hello, Donovan. I was just trying to grab a few minutes to call you. This morning the chief had one of the black and whites go out to the areas where the homeless folks set up camp." He snorted. "The tourists have no idea there's a homeless population here. And the city government likes it that way. Bad for tourism."

"Did they find anything?"

"They nosed around and found a guy fitting Emma's description. He ran, but the officers chased him down and arrested him without too much trouble."

"Thanks, Mike. Obviously, we're both pleased and relieved that an arrest has been made. I can't believe he's working alone though."

"That does seem unlikely to me too," Mike admitted. "Hopefully we'll know more after we interview him. Is Emma coming in to do an identification?"

"Yes, we'll be there at three." Donovan glanced at

his black and steel diver's watch, a gift from his grandfather when he had graduated from college. "We leave for the police station in about forty-five minutes."

"Good. I'll be back at the station by then. I'll see you there."

Donovan hung up the phone. "Let's see what happens this afternoon. If they've arrested your attacker, it's a step in the right direction."

Her voice filled with emotion. "It could be over soon."

Picking up her hand, he rubbed his thumb soothingly over her fist. "Yes. But I don't want you to get ahead of yourself. Mike said the guy they picked up is a vagrant. They haven't connected him to the drive-by shooting, and I don't know that they will be able to. It seems unlikely to me that this guy was acting alone. He sounds like a meth head. We need to know more about him. Is he truly itinerant, or was he just hiding among them? Because if he is down-and-out, he's unlikely to have a car. Which means he wasn't the shooter."

"Oh." Emma broke eye contact and folded in on herself.

Concerned at her reaction, he put an arm around her shoulder and drew her close. "Hey, now. I'm not trying to scare you. I just want you to continue to be cautious. I don't want you to get overconfident or sloppy with your personal safety."

She nodded but she didn't look up.

"Emma, look at me."

After a delay, she glanced at him. "This is good news. Don't doubt that. I just think that your assailant may be part of a bigger operation. So we need to keep our guard up. But I promise I will keep you safe." He paused. "Do you trust me to protect you?"

She met his gaze. "Yes, I do trust you."

Satisfaction darted across his face. "Good. We'll get to the bottom of this, and you'll get your life back. I promise."

Her phone pinged and she glanced down at the text message. "It's Ann-Marie. She's just checking if we're still going to the spa tomorrow. I forgot all about it. I guess I better cancel, huh?"

Donovan nodded. "It would be best until I can get a handle on things."

"I better fill Ann-Marie in on the drive-by shooting. I'm surprised she hasn't heard about it. She's hooked into the island grapevine like no one I know."

Donovan smirked. "I bet. Why don't you give her a call and update her and I'll do the same for Jack? Then we better head out to the police station."

"All right."

Leaning over, he kissed her lightly on the cheek. "I'll see you back down here in a few minutes. We'll need to leave in a half hour."

Chapter 13

Emma sat at the battle-scarred wooden conference table which filled the small room in the police station. Sergeant Mickler, in his crisply pressed uniform and high and tight haircut, sat opposite her. *He looks way too young for this job.* As if dealing a game of cards, he placed the mug shots on the table one by one. Emma frowned as she studied each photo in turn. "Definitely not those two photos." She flicked them out of the line with one finger.

"All right. How about the others? Take your time and look at the photos carefully."

"Hold it. That's him." Excited, she jabbed her finger on the sixth photo in the group.

"Are you positive?" Officer Mickler crossed his arms over his chest. "I need you to be completely sure. Your identification must stand up in court."

"Yes." She shivered and rubbed her arms. "That's definitely him. I'd recognize that face anywhere. Those sunken cheeks and beady eyes are burned in my mind." She blinked back tears. "I got a good look at him."

"All right. We appreciate you coming down today." Mickler gathered all the photographs and put them in a file. He pushed his chair back and stood.

"Wait! Is that all? Can you tell me if that is the man you have in custody?" Her throat closed as she recalled his foul smell as he lay on top of her, pressing

69

her into the bed.

He straightened and puffed out his chest. "Yes, it is. I'm sure the chief will brief you when it is appropriate to do so." He opened the door to the conference room. "I'll show you out."

Donovan stood as she approached. "How did it go?"

"I identified the man they arrested." She spoke very quietly.

Donovan put an arm around her shoulders and drew her in close to him. "That's great news. How about we go out to dinner to celebrate?"

Her cheeks grew warm. "Ah, I guess so. All right."

Her hesitation twisted his gut. *How can I get through to her? She clearly trusts me to protect her, but that's it.*

"Are you feeling well enough to go out? You haven't mentioned your throat or head hurting, so I assumed you were on the road to recovery?"

"I am feeling better. Being out and about takes my mind off it. Where did you have in mind?"

"How about that new restaurant, Ocean View? It was on a list of recommended eating places at my hotel."

"Perfect. They have rooftop tables and the view is amazing." *Maybe my life will get back to normal now. Who am I kidding? Going to dinner with Donovan is not my regular life.* Donovan took her arm and escorted her out of the police station. Opening the passenger door of his truck, he gave her a hand up.

Automatic doors swooshed open and closed behind them. The police chief lumbered out, hurrying toward him.

"Donovan, glad I—" He wheezed. "Glad I caught you. I wanted to personally thank you for doing your civic duty. My officer tells me you made a positive identification."

"Yes, *I did*." Emma bristled with irritation.

He inclined his head in her direction. "The city very much appreciates it. Please give my best to Jack." Emma fidgeted with her seat belt. Donovan put his hand on her arm. She understood his message clearly. *Don't make a fuss.*

"I will, Chief, thank you. And thanks to the officers who are working on my case."

"We're glad to help. Jack does a lot of fine work at Rutledge's. He cares about the community." Emma remained silent. *Must be time for reelection. Could he possibly be thinking of running against Ken? Can't wait for the solicitation of a donation to his campaign fund. He's kidding himself if he thinks Jack would back him against Ken.*

Donovan glanced at Emma. The silence grew uncomfortably long. "We appreciate your time, Chief. I better get Emma home. She's had a traumatic few days."

"Yes, sir. She surely has. Off you go." The chief slapped the side of the truck and waved them off.

Donovan started the engine, backed out of the parking space, and pulled away.

"That man is so odious. I can almost feel his eyes boring a hole in our backs." She wrinkled her nose as if he left a bad smell.

Donovan glanced briefly at her. "Take a deep breath. He may be a chauvinist, but we need to play nicely to ensure he updates us on this investigation." He

71

laughed. "That's not an easy ask. Trust me. I know."

She sighed loudly. "I know you're right. But his smalltown misogynistic attitude gets to me sometimes." She flexed her fists. "And frankly, that guy gives me the creeps."

They were stopped at a traffic light. He picked up her hand and kissed it. She hitched in a breath.

He laughed at her reaction. "Distracted you, huh?"

"Uh…yeah."

"Good. Let's not waste any more time on the chief." When the light changed, he pulled away.

"That's Ocean View in the distance."

"Looks like it's got the recipe for success. Less than a block from the ocean, with a rooftop bar. A great choice." The multi-story restaurant looked festive with its bright blue umbrellas on the rooftop. A line of casually dressed people extended out the door.

"Looks like there's a good sized crowd tonight. I don't see any open spaces out front, but if you drive around the back there should be some." She pointed to an alleyway behind the building. He followed her directions and found a parking space for the truck.

Joining the slow-moving queue of patrons, they waited to be seated on the rooftop patio. When they finally reached the front, the hostess, a blonde woman wearing a too snug "Ocean View" T-shirt and a miniskirt, stepped past Emma and threw her arms around Donovan.

"Well, look at you, honey!" She pulled back a little and beamed at him. "You sure done us proud in the military. I heard a rumor you were moving back home. I can see it must be true."

Donovan gently but firmly disengaged her arms

from around his neck. "Hello, Delores. It's been a long time. And yes, I've returned to the island. I've retired from the military."

Her eyes glinted. "We'll have to make sure your homecoming is memorable." Delores leaned in closer to Donovan. "What you gonna do? You got something lined up?" She fiddled with her hair, then trailed her finger down the V-neck of her T-shirt toward her cleavage.

"I may be joining Rutledge Commercial Properties."

At his words, Delores pouted. "Oh, Emma. I didn't see you there." Turning back to Donovan, she subtly arched her back to put her bosom front and center. "It's hard to move, even if it is home. I'd be happy to ease your transition." Her gaze lowered to his crotch.

"Thanks, Delores, but I'm fine." He was careful to keep his voice neutral. "If we could have a table on the roof that would be appreciated." He put his arm around Emma and pulled her into his side.

Delores' face tightened infinitesimally before smoothing out. She picked up menus and gestured with her hand. "Right this way." Not one to give up easily, she sashayed as she led them up the stairs.

Emma leaned in and whispered to Donovan, "An old friend?"

He shrugged. "Jack and I went to high school with her." He continued quietly, under cover of the ambient bar noise. "But that's it. I never dated her, nor gave her any reason to think I wanted to. You have nothing to worry about."

"Uh huh."

Delores led them to a high-top table along the

perimeter. The breeze off the ocean drifted across the open seating area, lifting a napkin that wasn't anchored with silverware. An optimistic seagull circled overhead in search of leftovers while a Jamaican steel band played a Bob Marley tribute. In the distance a cargo ship made its way up the coast.

"Would you like to order drinks?" Delores pulled out a notepad and pen.

Donovan tilted his head to the side. "I should have asked you earlier. Can you have alcohol, or are you still taking the pain medication?"

"I stopped taking the medicine." Emma looked up at Delores. "I'll have a glass of pinot grigio."

"House white, okay?" Delores scribbled on her notepad.

"Uh, sure."

Delores leaned over, and her breasts touched Donovan's upper arm. "What will you have, hon?" She pressed against him as she pointed to the beer list.

"I'll have an IPA."

"Sure, hon. You got it." Delores winked at him. "Your server will bring out your drinks shortly." She walked off, angling herself so that she was in Donovan's line of sight as she walked away.

Emma raised an eyebrow at him. "Well, someone has the hots for you."

Donovan narrowed his eyes. "Hey! I can't control her behavior. But I can control mine. Remember that."

"Got it." Emma straightened the silverware in front of her.

"We've wasted enough time gossiping about a high school acquaintance. Let's talk about something much more important."

"Ah sure. Do you think they have enough evidence to charge the man they arrested?"

"That wasn't the topic I was thinking about. I want to talk about us. You and me."

Irritated, she toyed with the menu, delaying her response. Finally, she set it down, aligning it squarely with the edge of the table. "There is no 'us.' That time has passed. Or maybe never was. I know long ago I wanted us to be together. But I moved on."

He cocked his head to the side. "So you're completely over me? You don't want to give us a try? See how we would be together?"

She shook her head. "It's not a good idea. It's the exact opposite. Bad. It's a very bad idea." Agitated, she gestured wildly to emphasize her point and knocked over the salt and pepper shakers. Her arm trembled as she picked them up. Rather than risk spilling anything else, she moved her hands off the table. However, still flustered, she fiddled with her paper napkin. A small mound of shredded napkin formed a pyramid in her lap. Finally, determined to put an end to her nervous fidgeting, she set the remnants of the napkin on the table and folded her hands.

"Hey." Donovan reached across the table and put his hand on her arm. At that moment, Delores returned and he pulled back. She slammed their drinks down. The foam from Donovan's beer spilled over the top of his glass. Delores walked away sharply.

He raised his beer to take a sip and grinned. "Message sent and received."

"Well played."

"Now, Emma, she wasn't catching the hint. I needed to be more obvious. But forget about anyone else. It's always been you. I'm sorry I waited so long to tell you." He swallowed the lump in his throat. "I realize now that it wasn't only my decision. I should have been more honest with you a long time ago."

"Yes, you should have." Adrenaline rushed through her body. "Now that you've decided you're ready for a relationship, I'm supposed to drop everything?" Her nostrils flared. Raw pain, long buried, seeped to the surface. She struggled to contain the tremors in her hand as she set her wine glass down.

A pained expression crossed his face, and he swallowed his frustration. "No. I don't expect anything." He scrubbed a hand over his face. "But I can hope. My hope is that you want to explore this thing between us as much as I want to." He paused. "I'm sorry, Emma. I'm truly sorry."

Clearly upset, she looked away, her chin trembling and her vision blurring. "I'm sorry." She swallowed. "I just can't deal with this right now, Donovan. It's just too much at the moment."

"I understand." Donovan's lips pressed together. "Can I ask just one thing?"

"I guess so." She stared at an object over his shoulder.

His chest tightened. "Please don't close the door on us." He reached out to touch her hand but pulled back. "Just think about it." He paused before continuing. "Promise me you'll think about it."

After a moment, she nodded. "I'll give it some consideration, Donovan. But no promises."

His mouth turned up slightly at the corners. She wasn't shutting him out. "That's all I ask."

She put a hand to the back of her head. Her head

throbbed. *This conversation isn't helping.* Her gaze flitted around the bar before returning to Donovan. *Time for a change of topic.* She cleared her throat. "On another subject, can you explain what will happen next in the criminal process?"

"Of course. The police will present the evidence to the district attorney's office. They'll file a complaint with the court. Within seventy-two hours, the defendant will be brought before the judge to enter a plea." He hesitated. "He'll also get a bond hearing at that point."

Emma inhaled sharply. "What! I just assumed he would be held until the trial. Will he be released?"

Donovan shook his head. "I don't know. Depends on a lot of factors. The seriousness of the charge, his ties in the community, whether he is a flight risk, etc. He's homeless, and it was a violent offense. I would think it unlikely that he would be released on a bond and that the judge would keep him detained. But you can never tell."

Her mouth fell open. "But he's dangerous!" Her voice shook. "Not only did he try to choke me and knock me out, but he also shot up Jack's house. That couldn't happen, could it? Tell me it can't." She covered her mouth with her hand.

"Unfortunately, at this point, there isn't any evidence to tie the shooting to your assault. Mike said they didn't find any weapons where he was camping."

"Damn. He probably ditched the gun. It would be the obvious thing to do. He may be a meth head, but he's not an idiot." Emma slumped in her chair.

"If it was him, he probably did get rid of the gun. But he doesn't have a vehicle registered to him. So, if he was the shooter it was stolen. Unless they find the vehicle, and it has his fingerprints, I don't know how they'll tie him to the shooting. Any half-witted criminal would swipe some wheels, and then burn them."

"He's going to get away with it, isn't he?" A tear leaked out and trickled down her cheek.

Donovan held her gaze. "I won't lie to you. It's possible the gunman may never be prosecuted. But I will promise you that I won't let anyone hurt you."

She blinked moisture away. "I know."

"Do you trust me?"

She fidgeted in her seat but didn't look away. "Yes."

Donovan's stomach churned. *That was the best he was going to get at the moment. It was something. It was a lot, actually. More than he deserved.*

"Come on. We'd better get some food in you before that wine goes to your head." He picked up a menu and handed it to her. She took it but immediately set it back down on the table.

"I'm embarrassed to say I know the options by heart. I'm going to have the shrimp salad. They do it well here."

When the waiter returned, Emma ordered the shrimp salad and Donovan asked for the seafood platter. Emma updated Donovan on local news while they waited for their food. After dinner, they took Zeus for his evening walk on the beach before heading upstairs to bed.

When they reached her door, Donovan paused. "I'm going to leave my door open. If you do the same, I'll be able to hear you if you call out."

"I'm not a fool—I won't argue about that. Thanks."

"Good." He leaned down and pressed his lips softly against hers. He tried to deepen the kiss, and she pulled away.

Donovan ran his finger down the side of her cheek. "I waited this long. I can wait a bit longer. I want to do this right. I want things to be good between us." Very gently, he pushed her hair off her face and kissed her.

"Goodnight, sweetheart. If you need anything, just call out."

"Goodnight." She pushed the door shut in his face but did not close it firmly.

Donovan's mouth twisted into a wry grimace. *All in good time.*

Without fully closing his door, he took off his clothes, leaving only his boxers on to sleep in. Then he got into bed, switched off the bedside light, and turned over to go to sleep.

Chapter 14

At breakfast the next morning, Donovan slathered marmalade on his toast. "Do you feel up to showing me the remaining condos?"

*He's not sure if I'm going to lose it showing a property.* Emma blew on her drink, took a sip, and set the mug down precisely in the center of the coaster. "Yes, of course. It would be better to keep busy. I'll just verify the scheduled appointments online with the other agent." She got up from the table. "I had better go do that right away. If the properties are occupied, the tenants can be fickle. If that is the case, we may not be able to get in today."

"Understood. While you do that, I'll take Zeus for a short walk. Don't open the doors for anyone, and keep your phone by your side."

"Isn't that a little overboard? It's broad daylight."

"No." He held her gaze for a moment until she looked away. He whistled. "Get your leash, Zeus."

At his command, Zeus trotted off to the laundry room and grabbed his tether in his mouth. After putting him on his lead, Donovan locked the back door behind them. They made their way down the wooden walkover which protected the sea oats and sand dunes. Once on the beach, he let the energetic dog off leash to sniff at his leisure and pulled his phone out of his pocket. With one eye on Zeus, who was christening some seaweed, he punched in a number. Jack picked up on the first ring.

"I just wanted to give you an update." Donovan explained everything that had happened.

"Thanks, Donovan. We'd like to stay a few more days in Atlanta. Ava's dad is doing better, but Ava is a big help to her mother."

"Understood. Everything is under control here. I'll give you a call if anything changes. Otherwise, I'll update you tomorrow." He whistled to Zeus. They wandered back up to the house and found Emma in the living room.

Eyes sparkling, she glanced up from her computer as they entered. "Good news. I've confirmed the viewings at those two condos, and I've also booked a mystery house."

"Hey, you look excited, kitten. What's up?" He sat on the arm of the sofa and looked over her shoulder. She grabbed his arm.

"How do you feel about a fixer upper?"

He reached over and tucked a wayward blonde curl behind her ear. *A project would be good for both of us. Give me a chance to use some of the skills Granddad taught me. And given Emma's enthusiasm, it would give us a chance to work together. To bond. If it takes a fixer-upper to grab her attention, then I'm all for it.* A smile tugged at his lips. "I hadn't thought about it, but I'm pretty handy with a hammer. So let's take a look at it."

She beamed. "Well, Jack could always lend you a construction crew if you don't want to do the work yourself. Here, take a look at this house." She turned the computer so he could see the screen. "If you like it,

81

we should probably jump on it. It will go fast. It's on the beachfront, just a half mile from here. It's been in one family and hasn't been updated in forty years. But the location is great, and it has good bones."

Donovan's brow furrowed as he flipped through the photographs in the listing. "I like the location. The long set-back from the road will help keep traffic noise down."

"Good points. And it's got curb appeal. A lot of people like the style of a two-story beach house with a wraparound porch."

He grimaced at the pictures of the inside. "The kitchen and bathrooms are vintage 1980s." He continued flipping the screen. "The living room has an amazing view of the ocean."

He stopped on the last picture and studied it. He tilted his head to the side. "If I fix it up, that will enhance the value of the property."

"Absolutely." Her face radiated enthusiasm. "We've got an appointment this morning. And we'll see the condos this afternoon. Ready?" She bounded up from her chair.

"Of course." A smile danced on his lips. *This house is a great distraction. For that reason alone, I'll love it.*

Emma grabbed her purse and computer. Donovan followed her out to the garage. After rummaging in her handbag, she pulled out her keys. "I don't think so." He closed her hand into a fist. "Put them away." He pulled his own keys out of his pocket. "I'll drive."

"I usually drive my clients." Her fingers bit into the strap of her bag.

"Not this one. I'm taking care of you."

An expression of sadness crossed her face, but she

put her car keys away. "All right. Are you going to leave the hurricane shutters secured?"

"Yes. No harm in having them down. It's safer that way."

With a quick press on the button on his key fob, Donovan unlocked his truck and helped Emma in. He climbed in the driver side and glanced at her.

He glanced at her. "Where to?"

"151 Ocean Avenue. Make a right out of the driveway. It's half a mile on the right side."

Donovan backed out of the garage, pulled onto the road, and followed her directions. Glimpses of blue peeked out between the ocean-side properties as they drove. He sped up to pass a garbage truck lurching between neighboring trash cans. After a beach access parking lot he pulled into the driveway of a bright blue beach house. He parked and switched off the engine but made no move to get out of the car. He studied the house carefully.

Idly tapping his finger on his thigh, he gazed at the property. He cocked his head as he contemplated the structure.

She watched him while he studied the house. "What does that expression mean?"

His mouth tilted up at the corners. "It means I'm thinking. Which is exactly what I'm doing. Could I put a fence and gate in the front of the property for a dog to run loose?"

"Of course. There is no homeowner's association on Ocean Avenue. So there is no need for permission, other than the usual building permits of course. And those are just a matter of paying the city a fee."

He stroked his chin. "Let's go see what the inside

holds. Ready to re-visit the 1980s?"

"You may need to invest in an exotic car." She chuckled. "Do you remember the movie? *Back to the Future*?"

"Of course. A classic. But I don't think I'm ready for time travel."

"Come on." She gestured toward the house. "Better keep that sense of humor. You may need it. Just remember—if all it requires are cosmetic changes, those are easy to make. Don't be put off by the appearance. And even walls can be moved depending on how the house was framed."

A gravel path curved around landscape beds filled with mona lavender plants, and led to the front door. The purple flowers contrasted with the deep green of the mondo grass. A lizard did several pushups before scurrying under the canopy of the ground cover. The crushed rock crunched under their feet as they approached the house.

Emma opened the lock box to get the key out. When she turned the handle and pushed, the door remained firmly shut. "Ugh. It's stuck. Darn humid Florida weather. The timber expands."

"I know. I'd forgotten that. I used to have to plane a little off my grandparents' door on a regular basis."

She glanced quickly at him. "You must miss them."

He nodded curtly. "Like your parents, they'll always be with us. Here, let me give it a try." He twisted the handle and used his shoulder to press against the door. The wood groaned but gave way. "Lead the way."

They stepped inside. He blinked. "Whoa."

Bemused, he stared at the garish plum carpet that covered the open plan living area.

Her confidence wavered. She put a hand on his arm. "Remember what I said. This living space is great." She pointed to the adjacent kitchen. "And it's a wonderful floor plan for entertaining. Come on. Let's explore outside." She unlatched the sliding glass door which opened up to a cracked concrete patio.

"It's a good size backyard." She tapped a finger against her mouth. "You could take up this concrete, lay pavers, and maybe put in an outdoor kitchen."

He clasped his hands behind his back and surveyed the area. "That would make this space ideal for entertaining."

"There's even room for a plunge pool if you wanted one. Can you picture it? Right here." She walked the length of the patio, counting as she stepped. "See? Definitely large enough."

"It's worth considering. Does Jack have a pool contractor that he would recommend?"

Emma guffawed. "Of course. Jack has a contractor for everything. Come on, let's see the rest of the house."

She took his hand and pulled him back inside. "The owner's suite is on the ground floor." Down the hall, she opened a door at the midway point. "This is the half bathroom."

Donovan peered over her shoulder and cringed. An avocado green sink and toilet clashed with the harvest gold floor tiles. "You've got to be kidding me. I don't know which color is worse."

She held her hands up in front of her. "I know. I know. The color choices are pretty awful. But imagine if you gutted this bathroom. You would have a blank canvas. You could make it anything you wanted."

"Yes. It would definitely need to be stripped." They continued on down the hallway to the main bedroom.

Emma twirled around; hands open wide. "Just look at the possibilities. A king size bed would fit in here." Opening one of the closet doors, she peeked inside. "Hmm…The closets are a bit small."

She looked around thoughtfully. "You could afford to shrink this area a little to enlarge the closets."

"Let's see what other surprises are in store for us." She opened the bathroom door and flicked on the light. She grimaced but quickly smoothed her face out. "It's a decent size. Rip out the bathtub and put in a generous size shower. There is already a 'his and her' vanity so you would only need to update it."

He looked over her shoulder. "Someone really liked avocado green. But you're right. This should be a fairly straightforward remodel." He followed her back into the bedroom.

She smiled broadly as she pointed to the sliding glass door. "Can you imagine waking up to the sunrise?" He watched her face light up with enthusiasm as she looked out the window.

"Shall we look upstairs?" She pulled his arm toward the stairs.

"Of course. I can't wait to see the rest of the house."

"You should definitely buy this place." Her cheeks started to burn, and she pressed her hands to her face. "Sorry. Sometimes I let my enthusiasm get the better of me."

"Hey, don't apologize. I'm glad you like the house. That's important to me." He cast her a veiled glance.

A flash of irritation crossed her face. "Don't go there, Donovan. Come on." She hurried up the stairs.

"This is advertised as a four-bedroom house, but the fourth bedroom would make a nice office." They entered a double-size room. "A 'Jack and Jill' bathroom leads into a second, slightly smaller guest room. And across the hall is the last bedroom, which overlooks the ocean.

"This would make a perfect office for you. You could put a desk here." She gestured to one end of the room. "From this window you could watch all the activity on the beach. The asking price is very reasonable since it needs major renovations. A lot of people are put off by the cost and inconvenience caused by modifying a house. And the market has been a bit slow."

He rubbed the stubble on his chin. "I can see the advantages to this property over the condo I viewed with Jack. It would be good for a family in due course."

Emma stared at her feet. Anger boiled up inside her. Was that comment meant for her? For them? Or was it idle talk about whatever future he had? With whomever? He was so free and easy with his words. *Typical Donovan. He was always the one in control. He sets the rules. He makes the decisions.*

He reached out toward her but pulled back and jammed his hands in his pockets. "Hey, you've gone very quiet."

She squared her shoulders. "Uh, yes, sorry. I just lost my train of thought for a moment. You were saying?"

"I'd like to put an offer in on this house for ten thousand under the asking price, since it's a sluggish market. What do you think?"

She glanced at him before her gaze darted away. "That's a great offer. Even at full price, it's a good deal. Let's go back to Jack's and do the paperwork. Then I'll present the offer. While we wait for a response, we can get lunch. I do suggest we view the other condos in case your offer isn't accepted or the home inspector finds an expensive problem when he does the inspection."

"That makes sense."

They went back out to Donovan's truck and headed back to Jack's house.

Chapter 15

Emma hit the send button on the e-mail to the seller's agent with the written offer to buy the house. "There, that's done. Let's get lunch."

Donovan's stomach gurgled. "I guess I'm hungry."

"Let me see what I can find to eat." Emma hunted around in the refrigerator, pulling out sandwich fillings. She glanced over her shoulder. "Are you feeling adventurous?"

Donovan smirked.

She made a face. "No, not that. Men have one-track minds. I was wondering if you wanted to try Elsa's faux tuna salad. It's made with chickpeas and celery.

"I'm easy."

"Don't flirt with me, Donovan. I said I wasn't ready, and I'm not." Exasperated, she slapped mustard on a slice of bread.

He held his hands up. "Sorry. A guy can hope, can't he?"

"Right now, I need you to focus on lunch."

His mouth twitched. "I'll try the faux tuna. I've eaten a lot of strange things in the military. Faux tuna is nothing."

"Great. Because that's what you're getting." She spread the chickpea mixture on whole wheat bread. After layering lettuce and sliced tomatoes, she cut the sandwiches and put them on plates. She added sliced apples on the side and set the plates on the breakfast bar with glasses of water.

"Looks good. Thank you." He took a large bite, chewed, and swallowed. "Hmm…it's not a bad taste. Not sure I'd call it tuna though."

"Well, I'm glad you like it." She bit into a piece of apple. "Do you miss it?"

"Miss what?" He broke off a piece of his sandwich and slipped it to Zeus under the table. He pretended not to notice when Zeus spit the food out.

Emma leaned back in her chair. "The Navy."

He took a sip of water. "Yeah, sure. I miss it. The guys I served with were my family for many years. I hope we'll always keep in touch. There was always something exciting happening, either with my trial work or a deployment. But time marches on, and I was ready for the next phase of my life."

She picked up their empty plates and loaded them in the dishwasher. "Come on. We had better get moving if we want to see those condos."

Chapter 16

"This first property is a few blocks in from the beach. It's still only a short walk to the water. There's no garage, but you would have a dedicated carport space under the building."

Donovan gazed at the building, taking in the three-story flat-roofed structure. An external staircase led to the rooftop which had been converted to patio space. He gestured to the scattering of chairs. "I bet there's a great view from up there."

"That's one of the attractions of this condo."

They took the outside stairs to the second-floor unit. She opened the lockbox and unlocked the condo.

"It's a bit dreary in here." His brows drew together. "Any way to get more light in here? What about a sun tube in the ceiling?"

She pushed a curl behind her ear. "Unfortunately not."

"It is what it is?"

"I'm afraid so. You can make internal modifications but not any external changes such as putting in a skylight, etc." She pointed to the wall. "The dark paint doesn't help."

"Copy that."

Emma shifted her weight, watching him. "This is listed as a two bedroom with study." Walking down the hallway to the owner's suite, she continued her sales patter. "This is a spacious room. What do you think?" She turned around, but he was nowhere to be seen. Resigned to the quirks of clients, she went back to the living room.

"I don't think this one would work for me." He scowled. "It reminds me of a military barracks I once stayed in. Same gloomy look."

She made a face. "Tell me how you really feel. But there is no need to waste time here if it doesn't call out to you. When you know, you know. Let's go to the second condo."

"Sounds like a plan." Donovan held the door open for Emma to precede him. A wall of humid air carried the sweet scent of the wisteria that grew up the side of the building as they made their way back to Donovan's vehicle.

He started the engine. "Where to now?"

She read the address from her notes and directed him to turn north on Ocean Avenue. A family of four weekend cyclists wobbling on their bicycles veered into the road, and Donovan swerved to avoid them. He swore quietly.

Emma smirked. "You've been away too long. You've forgotten the first rule of tourism. Beware the tourists. They behave irrationally."

"Yeah, it would be funny. Except it's not. They're dangerous."

She sighed. "That's life on the island. Turn there." Donovan pulled into the parking lot. The four-story condo faced the beach. Red and pink oleander bushes splashed color against the white building. "This looks more promising. And I like that every unit has a balcony facing the ocean."

"Good. Let's go inside. The condominium for sale is on the fourth floor."

Donovan glanced at her. "Elevator or stairs?"

"Oh, stairs, definitely. I can sneak in some exercise."

Emma's chest rose and fell rapidly and sweat beaded on her forehead as they climbed several flights of stairs. She slanted a glance at Donovan. His chest was barely moving. *Back to the gym. I need to stop avoiding the Stairmaster.* Emma opened the door. "After you." Panoramic windows the length of the living room overlooked the ocean. A cohort of pelicans formed a perfect line as they skimmed over the waves, dipping down and rising above as if their journey had been choreographed. The gentle swell of the water could easily lull viewers into a trance.

Emma's eyes widened. "That's impressive."

"Yeah, that's quite an outlook." Donovan walked over to the window. "You could have breakfast on the balcony and watch the sunrise." Donovan clasped his hands easily behind his back as he looked around thoughtfully. "I'm impressed so far. What do you think of it?"

"It doesn't matter what I think." She cleared her throat. "You're the one who would be living here."

An emotion that might have been regret passed briefly over Donovan's face. "Let's see what else it has going for it."

"Good." Emma gestured for him to precede her down the hallway. "This is a half bath. Now let's go see the owner's suite."

"Huh." He crossed his arms over his chest. "It's a generous sized bedroom and bathroom."

She flung the door to the guest room open. "Take a look in here." She looked at Donovan. "Well, what do you think?"

"It's nice." He shrugged half-heartedly. "It's a possibility. But the beach house is my favorite, and then the condo I saw with Jack. And to be honest, I don't look forward to going up and down four flights of stairs every time my dog has to go out."

She rolled her eyes. "You don't have a dog."

He flashed a grin. "Not yet, true. But soon."

"Well, I'm glad you have a couple possibilities. We should hear from the seller's agent soon on the house."

"All right. Let's go back to Jack's."

Just then, Donovan's phone beeped. He opened the text message and read it quickly.

"It's from Mike. The case is set for arraignment and a bail hearing tomorrow at ten."

Emma inhaled sharply. She put her hand on the doorway to support herself.

"Can we go? I want to see that bastard in handcuffs." An icy chill ran down her spine. "I want to take some of my power back."

Pleased that she was handling the news well, he pulled her into a hug and kissed her hair before she had a chance to pull back. "Of course. If you think that would help you, then we'll go. It should be open to the public."

Chapter 17

The next morning, raindrops splattered the windscreen. The automatic wipers increased in frequency as the clouds opened up. Donovan pulled into a parking space in front of the red brick courthouse on Main Street in downtown Victoria City. The still-dark shopfronts on either side were devoid of customers. The bells in the tower peeled loudly on the quarter hour. Emma hunched, her arms crossed over her stomach. He rubbed her shoulder gently. "Hey, it's okay if you changed your mind. No one will think less of you if you don't want to see him."

She swallowed, but the sour taste in her mouth didn't go away. Exhaling, she sat back against the seat and uncrossed her arms. "Let's do this."

Donovan squeezed her hand. "It's normal to dread this. You're not alone. Every victim I've ever interviewed when I was a prosecutor had some sort of visceral reaction when they saw their attacker. I'll be with you the whole time."

"Thanks." She reached for the truck door.

The sun, obscured by dark clouds, cast a pall over the downtown. They dodged between puddles, hurrying to the shelter of the building's overhang. Donovan lifted her chin with one finger. "Hey, you've got this."

A sad look on her face, Emma shook water off her clothes. When she finished, he held the door open for her.

"Hi, Martin. How are you?" Fluorescent strip lights, incongruous with the historic architecture, reflected off the silver-gray hair of the security guard.

"Hello, Emma. I heard what happened to you." He shook his head side to side. "Just terrible. Terrible. I'm surely glad to see you feeling better."

"Thanks, Martin. I appreciate the kind words." She gestured to Donovan who was directly behind her. "You must remember Donovan Evans?"

Donovan reached out and shook his hand. "Hello, Martin. It's been a long time since you coached varsity."

"I remember you well, Donovan. You played some terrific high school football. You made the whole island proud."

Donovan laughed. "Thanks. Good to see you again."

"You're here for the Miller hearing, I take it?"

"Yes, sir."

"That's in courtroom C. Third door on the right."

Emma opened her purse. Martin glanced inside and waved them through the metal detector.

Once through the security screening, they proceeded down the hallway to the appropriate courtroom. Donovan held the door open for Emma and followed her into the room. He steered her toward the back. Already a number of people sat in the area set aside for the public. "I'm just going to have a quick word with the prosecutor." Squeezing past several people, Emma took a seat at the end of the row while Donovan made his way to the front.

The door in the back opened, and Ann-Marie

sauntered in. Heads turned, and quiet murmurs hummed in the public gallery. Her short, flirty dress and high-heeled sandals showed off her toned legs. She thrust her way through to sit next to Emma and enveloped her in a hug.

"Thanks for coming," Emma whispered.

"I wouldn't have missed it for anything, sugar. I wanted to be here to support you."

Emma squeezed her hand.

"Where's Donovan?"

Emma pointed to the prosecutor's table, where he was talking to the government's attorney.

In the front of the room, Donovan explained his connection to Emma to the official. "Do you expect the judge to grant bail?"

The assistant district attorney for Victoria County stood and adjusted the jacket of his slightly worn suit. He shuffled his pile of overstuffed files until he found Miller's file. As he flipped through the top pages, skimming the contents, he shook his head. "He shouldn't. The defendant doesn't have a fixed address. That alone should disqualify him from release. I'll be asking that he be held in custody for that reason, and because it was a violent offense. I do expect the judge to set a bond, although it will probably be high. This judge tends to split the difference." He gestured with his arms open and palms up.

"Well, at least it should be substantial. I don't know if the police told you, but the house where Emma is staying was hit by gunfire. The incidents have to be related."

The attorney glanced up from his paperwork. "Do you have any evidence that they're connected?"

"Not yet."

"Pity." The prosecutor went back to organizing his papers. "That would keep him detained for sure."

"Emma is here if you need any testimony."

"Thanks. We always appreciate cooperative witnesses. The judge is unlikely to allow that, though."

"I thought not. I appreciate your time." He walked to the back of the room where Emma sat and nodded to Ann-Marie.

Emma's heart drummed. "What did he say?"

"He thinks the judge will grant bail, but it will be a large amount since Miller seems to be homeless." *The less said the better.*

A side door opened, and a prison guard came in leading three prisoners in orange jump suits with "VCJ" stenciled in black letters on the back. Handcuffs clanging, they shuffled in unison to bench seating at the side of the room. A second jailer brought up the rear.

Sweat trickled down Emma's spine even as a blast from the air conditioner swept through the room. Miller was the last defendant. His jail uniform hung on his emaciated frame. His hands were cuffed in front of him. *He can't hurt me now. He can't hurt me now. He can't hurt me now. Mantras are becoming my thing.* She stifled a hysterical giggle at the thought. Donovan put his hand on her leg, gently soothing her.

The prisoners sat and the guards removed their shackles. Miller scanned the courtroom. His gaze drifted past Emma, then returned. He shot her a look full of venom.

She froze, rooted to her seat. Donovan stroked her thigh, and she flinched at the heaviness of his hand. He leaned sideways and whispered, "Just look away. Keep your attention on the front of the courtroom."

She stared at him like a deer caught in headlights. *This is probably how people get bitten by snakes. Hypnotized into paralysis.*

"You okay?" Donovan whispered.

"Yes." Her red face and brittle response belied the truth of her statement. She folded her hands together in her lap and concentrated on looking forward.

"All rise. The honorable Judge Edwin Atwell presiding." The bailiff's voice boomed over the buzz of conversation. They stood and waited for the judge to come in.

The door opened, and a white-haired narrow-faced man in black judicial robes that flapped loosely on his skeletal frame shuffled in. He ambled slowly up the steps to the bench and sat. Judge Atwell scanned the courtroom over his half-rim black glasses and banged his gavel.

"Order. Order in the court." Her throat closed as he slammed his gavel again for good measure. "Call the first case, bailiff."

The bailiff flipped through the paperwork on his clipboard. "The court calls State v. Robert Miller."

The guard pointed to a chair at the defendant's table. Miller shuffled over and sat down.

The judge rifled through the paperwork for several minutes then raised his head and peered at Miller over the top of his glasses. "Sir, do you have an attorney?"

"No." Robert Miller's sunken cheeks caved in farther as he spoke. The officer leaned over and said something sharply to Miller.

He stood. "No, Your Honor."

"That's better. All right. I'll explain the charges

against you." The judge shuffled through his file before pulling out several pages. "Ah. Here it is."

"Your honor, your honor, George Cantwell for the defense." An eloquent voice with a hint of an Atlanta accent rang out. A man carrying a hand-tooled leather briefcase hurried from the back to the defense table and stood next to Miller. Once he set his attaché down, he unbuttoned the jacket of his custom-tailored suit. Judge Atwell's gaze shifted from Cantwell to Miller.

"Mr. Miller, is this your attorney?"

Robert Miller glanced at the expensively dressed, slick lawyer and shrugged. "I guess he must be."

"Very well. Proceed, Mr. Cantwell."

Smoothing his tie with manicured hands, Cantwell cleared his throat. "Your honor, the defendant waives reading of the charges and would like to enter a plea of not guilty. My client would also like to put a bail application forward."

"So noted. Mr. Marsh, what is the bond set at? I don't see it in my paperwork."

The prosecutor stood and buttoned his suit jacket. "Your honor, because this is a violent offense, and the defendant does not own any property, the state requests that he be held without bond. He is a flight risk."

The judge looked at defendant's counsel.

"Mr. Cantwell, what do you have to say?"

Cantwell put his hand on Miller's arm as he spoke. "Your honor, Mr. Miller is a valued and longstanding member of the community." Heads of several people sitting in the back of the courtroom bobbed in agreement as Cantwell spoke. "The High Road Church has come forward to offer Mr. Miller a place to stay, employment, and anger management counseling. They have agreed to be responsible for him and will ensure his appearance at all proceedings."

Emma shifted in her seat and glanced anxiously at Donovan. He squeezed her hand.

"That's a generous offer from the church, Mr. Cantwell." The judge scrutinized the people seated in the back of the courtroom. "Is anyone from the church here?"

"Yes, your honor. Pastor Chuck Freeman is here with some of his congregation." Cantwell gestured to a man wearing a faded tan sport coat and trousers in the front row of the visitor seating. The minister hoisted himself to his feet.

"Pastor Freeman, is what the defendant's attorney said true?"

Pastor Freeman's focus shifted to Miller for a moment before returning to the Judge. His face, half hidden behind his salt and pepper beard, glowed with the light of a true believer in his cause. "Yes, Your Honor. The church is ready, willing, and able to support our lost brother. Many in my congregation have come forward and are anxious to help Mr. Miller with his rehabilitation." He gestured to the row behind him.

Judge Atwell took off his glasses and nibbled on one of the arms before putting them back on. He peered at the clergyman. "Can you ensure that he attends all his court appearances?"

"Yes, Your Honor." The pastor shifted his weight.

"Very well. I'll release the defendant into the custody of the church." He banged his gavel.

"What! How can you do that?" She sprang to her feet. "That's outrageous! He's dangerous. You can't release him! Look at the bruises on my throat! He did this!"

A collective gasp erupted from the congregation.

"Quiet in the courtroom." The judge banged his gavel. He pointed at Emma. "You are out of order." The bailiff started toward her.

"Let's get out of here," Donovan whispered to Emma. He ushered her and Ann-Marie out the back of the courtroom and shut the door noiselessly behind him.

"Of all the crazy decisions. I can't believe he did that." She covered her mouth with her hand as she fought a wave of nausea.

"I'm sorry, sweetheart. It's a terrible decision." He rubbed her back.

"Can the prosecutor do anything? Is there an appeal?"

"A judge has a lot of latitude in setting bond. To be honest, that's probably a waste of time." His fingernails scored his palms. *How on earth did the High Road Church get involved?*

"Donovan, he'll be free to come after me again." Her voice quivered, and she wrapped her arms around herself.

"Look at me, Emma." He put his hands on her shoulders to get her attention, but her gaze continued to dart around the lobby of the courthouse like a panicked deer. He shook her gently but firmly.

She looked up at him. Wide-eyed. Distraught.

He spoke through gritted teeth. "I won't let anything happen to you. Ever. He won't get near you. You have my word on that."

"I believe you mean that." She hesitated. "But I'm afraid. I can't bear it that I'm afraid of that nasty old man. I hate that he's taken my security away from me."

"That's normal, honey. But if you're scared, you'll be careful."

"I'm glad you're here, Donovan. Not just because of that crazy man."

He put his arm around her and kissed her cheek. "I'll be here for as long as you'll let me." He held her until she stopped shaking.

Ann-Marie reached over to smooth Emma's hair. "I can see you're in good hands. I'll let Donovan take care of you, and I'll check in with you later. I've got to go open the salon."

"Thanks. I appreciate you coming down here," Emma whispered.

"Come on. Let's get out of here." He led her out of the building, waving to Martin as he opened the door to leave. They returned to Donovan's truck. He put the key in the ignition but didn't turn it. Instead, he sat looking forward. "I'm so sorry this happened, Emma."

She managed a wan smile for a moment, but it disappeared quickly. "You're not responsible. You didn't let that maniac loose." Icy shards slammed into her brain. Memories of Miller choking her flooded her mind. She shook her head as if to stop the flashbacks. "I will get through this. With your help."

His hands eased on the steering wheel. "Let's go home."

"Let me check for any messages." She turned her phone back on, and it beeped. "Just give me a minute to listen to these."

"Of course." Donovan scanned their surroundings. *Old habits die hard.*

She methodically listened to each message, then turned to Donovan.

103

"Good news." She fiddled with her phone, her voice flat. Donovan swore silently. Miller's release had set back Emma's recovery. "Your offer has been accepted. The house is yours."

"That's wonderful news." He ran his finger down her cheek. "It will make a great home." He paused. "I hope you'll help me with the renovations."

"Of course. We're friends. All the Rutledges will help you."

He stifled a sigh. *Backpedaling.* "And the other messages?"

"Oh, yes. Another bit of good news. Ava called and said her father is doing better. He's being released from the hospital, but she and Jack are going to stay in Atlanta for a few more days. And the final voicemail was a reminder for a continuing education course I signed up for tomorrow." She forced enthusiasm into her voice. "But enough about that. Let me set up the house inspection. We'll want to know what issues that house has."

"That sounds good. Do you have someone reliable?"

"Of course. Rutledge Commercial Properties has an excellent person on retainer. I'll get him out there tomorrow. It's good to get it done quickly since the inspection period is only ten days."

"I'd appreciate you setting that up." Donovan smiled at her briefly then steered the truck toward the south end of the island. They reached Jack's house, and Donovan parked in the garage.

"I'm going to make a quick phone call while you contact Jack's man." Donovan ran up the stairs two at a time and closed his door behind him.

He punched the button for Mike.

"Hey, man. I've been trying to get in touch with you. Miller made bail this morning."

"I know. We just got back from the hearing. Judge Atwell has lost it. Miller's homeless, a drug addict, and violent, for crying out loud. Emma almost exploded in the courtroom when she heard his decision. For a minute, I was worried Judge Atwell was going to lock her up for contempt."

Mike snorted. "That would have been quite a shit storm. It was unlucky that the case was on Atwell's docket. That old man has made some crazy decisions, and they're only getting nuttier as time goes on. He should have retired twenty years ago."

"Clearly." Donovan bit the words out. "But it's the decision, and we're stuck with it. I'm going to stay with Emma day and night. I wouldn't put it past Miller, or whoever is pulling his strings, to come after her again. On another note, what do you know about this High Road Church? They've agreed to be responsible for Miller."

"High Road Church? That's a small church on the north end of the island. I don't know much about them. They're pretty new. They took over an abandoned warehouse, and some of them live in the 'church.' I don't know anyone who goes there. I occasionally get some complaints because they solicit house to house. But they've always seemed harmless enough."

"Good to know. Thanks." Donovan hesitated a moment. "Keep me updated on the police investigation?"

"Always. Take care, man," Mike responded.

"You, too." Donovan hit the end button. He went

downstairs in search of Emma. He found her in Jack's office, sitting at the side desk. While she flipped through her appointment book, she chewed on her pen. She glanced up when he walked in.

"Good news. I've got Rupert scheduled to inspect your house tomorrow."

"Great. Can I be there, or will that be a problem?"

"It depends on the inspector. But I'm sure it will be fine with Rupert. Fair warning. He's a bit of a character."

"Oh? How so?"

"Well, he always, and I mean always, dresses in these loud plaid pants. And he'll talk your ear off. But Jack has used him for years and trusts his judgment. And because he needs to keep on Jack's good side, he'll do a thorough job for you."

Donovan laughed. "Consider me warned. I don't mind if he is a little eccentric as long as he is diligent and competent."

"His inspection will definitely be comprehensive. I would attend as well, but I've got a seminar tomorrow."

"You said that earlier. Where and when?"

"It's at the Community Center, near downtown. It's all day, nine to four."

"Will you be in that building the entire time?"

"Yes, they serve lunch and have a speaker during that time. I'll be with people every minute."

"All right. That sounds safe. I'll drop you off in the morning and pick you up at four. You should absolutely stay in the building with people all day. Don't leave the building for any reason. I'll come get you when it's over."

"Yes, sir." She saluted him.

"I mean it, Emma." He sat down next to her on the sofa and leaned close, his face only inches from hers.

"What?" She pulled away from him.

He leaned in and kissed her gently. Her mouth softened under his.

Memories inundated her. Donovan hanging around with Jack. Summer parties at the beach. Donovan at her graduation party. She had loved Donovan for the longest time. Of course, she had tried to dismiss her feelings as those of an immature girl. But she knew better. She had wanted this for so long. But still she hesitated.

He could feel her slight jerk and broke off the kiss. "Still not quite ready, huh? No problem, sweetheart. We have all the time in the world." He paused. "I don't know about you, but I could use some food. And after lunch, how about a walk on the oceanfront with Zeus?"

"Thanks," she whispered.

"For what?"

"For not being mad."

He ran a finger down her cheek. "I don't know what kind of jerks you've been dating, but if a lady is not ready, she's not ready. We can take this slow, Emma. I'm a patient man." He paused. "As long as I know I'll be getting what I want in the end."

Anger blazed in her face, and she snapped, "I'm not sure that's being patient." She turned away and forced an upbeat tone. "About lunch. I make a 'to die for' grilled cheese sandwich. Elsa usually has homemade soup in the freezer."

"The way to a man's heart is through his stomach. You're well on track, sweetheart."

Her cheeks flamed at his comment. "Please don't

say things like that, Donovan."

The corners of his mouth turned down, but he kept his voice neutral. "I'll try not to."

She opened the refrigerator and pulled out multiple types of cheeses. She glanced over her shoulder. "I hope you like artisan cheese. Elsa picks up some unique flavors at the Farmer's Market. I usually just throw a couple into the sandwich and see what happens. How about an English style cheddar with onions and locally made cranberry chutney?"

"I'm sure it will taste great. To be brutally honest, there isn't much I don't eat."

"Well, that should make it easy." She took out a plastic container of Elsa's roasted red pepper and tomato soup. Next to the fridge was the breadbox where she found whole wheat bread to add to her stockpile of ingredients. Another cabinet yielded what she sought. "Aha. The panini maker. Right where I left it the last time I used it."

"I'm going to take Zeus out. Back in a few minutes." Donovan whistled to the dog, and they went out the back door toward the sandy embankment.

By the time Donovan and Zeus returned, the aroma of caramelized onions and cheese filled the kitchen. She plated the sandwiches and ladled soup into bowls.

"Here, let me do that for you." Donovan carried their food to the kitchen table.

He took a large bite of the sandwich. She idly cut up her sandwich.

"Penny for your thoughts?"

She started and shook her head. "Uh, sorry. I guess my mind was just wandering."

"They didn't look like happy thoughts." He paused.

"Were you worrying about Miller?"

"Um, yes, that was it."

He put his hand over hers. "It's only natural to be anxious. But I won't let anything happen to you."

"I know." But she jerked her hand away, picked up their plates, and put them in the dishwasher. She wiped at an imaginary spot on the granite counter so hard her arm ached.

"Why do I get the feeling it's not really Miller that's bothering you?" Donovan got up and stood behind her. His breath tickled the back of her neck. He spoke, but she didn't turn around.

He put his hands on her arms to stop her cleaning. "Talk to me, Emma. What's wrong?"

Sighing, she put down the rag.

"It's all been a bit much." The dam of emotion broke, and the words flooded out. "You've spent fifteen years ignoring me, and now you act like you want a future with me. That's quite a turnaround. I've been on an emotional roller coaster since you returned. I'm having trouble wrapping my head around this." The anger boiled up inside her.

His face softened. "Actually, it hasn't been a turnaround." He paused, trying to find words to explain his feelings. Not something he was particularly good at. "I've wanted you since you turned eighteen. No, that's not quite accurate. It started even before that. You grieved for your parents, and I wanted to hold you. I remember you leaving for your prom. I was shooting pool with Jack at the time. You were seventeen and wore a pink dress. I wanted to be the one to take you to the dance. But I was too old for you. I remember your high school graduation. You were so beautiful and

109

happy in your cap and gown. You had college and your future ahead of you. I was jealous of the boys you would date. You were home from the university, and we played volleyball. The difference in our ages has always kept me back. And then it was the military. It didn't seem fair to you to have a long-distance relationship. And to have you wonder if I would come back or be killed. Although I wasn't on the front lines, I was stationed overseas and was still in harm's way. It's you, Emma. It's always been you for me. No one else ever measured up to your beauty, your intelligence, your kindness."

Emotion overwhelmed her. She closed her eyes, but the tears leaked out and ran down her face.

"It isn't your unilateral choice to decide when to have a relationship." The words flew out of her mouth. She wiped the moisture from her face. "I just need a little time to make the adjustment." She paused, then confessed, "There hasn't been anyone else for me either."

He gathered her in his arms and pulled her against his chest.

"I know this is a big change for us both. We'll take it as slow as you need to. I mean it, Emma. Whatever it takes."

She mumbled against his shirt, "And if it takes me months to come around?"

He tilted her chin up. "I've waited years for you Emma. I'll wait the same again." He paused. "But obviously I don't want to wait any longer than I have to. But you're in the driver seat."

She swallowed hard and wiped the tear tracks with the backs of her hands.

He gentled his voice. "How about that walk on the beach?"

She nodded. "That would be great."

Chapter 18

Donovan dropped Emma at the Community Center for her workshop the next morning just before nine. He waited in the parking lot until she was safely inside, then reversed and headed back to Ocean Avenue and "his" house. His limbs tingled as energy zinged through his body. *A place to call home.* He turned into the long driveway. A white pickup with a magnetic "Rutledge Properties" sign on the side was parked in front of the garage. He pulled up next to it and got out of his truck.

It was a cloudless blue sky, perfect conditions to make his beach house look extra appealing. The sun warmed the paved path which meandered through random groupings of plants. A pair of osprey soared above the waves hoping to spot the unlucky fish that would constitute their first meal of the day. A fresh breeze off the ocean cooled him as he approached the house. A lightness spread through his chest. This felt right. This was his house. *This is home.*

A man in shockingly loud red plaid pants stood by the front door.

Donovan held his hand out. "You must be Rupert."

"That I am. I'm excited to inspect this property. I've been in the business for over thirty years." He laughed self-deprecatingly. "But I've never had the opportunity to look around this house." He grinned. "My missus says I'm nosy. Maybe she's right." He

112

grabbed a white one-piece jumpsuit out of the back of his truck, stepped into it, and zipped it up. "Let's get started." He unloaded a large toolbox on wheels from his truck and headed to the front door.

Then he took out a computer and opened up a program to take notes. "I usually start with the exterior. I'm going to crawl underneath the house and look at the structure. And also check for termites."

"Sounds good." When he saw the size of the aperture, Donovan laughed. "I'll wait here. That crawlspace doesn't look very big or inviting to a guy my size."

Rupert looked up at him. "You're not wrong on that. But not many homeowners want to actually go underneath the house. Most are more than happy to take my word."

While Rupert began his work, Donovan sat on the front steps within shouting distance. He opened his computer and hit the power. It booted up, and he typed "High Road Church" into the search bar. His results popped up, and he scrolled through them. The church had 501(c)(3) federal tax-exempt status. A social media page showed some of the congregation organizing a food drive. Their website listed multiple services on Sunday and bible study classes on Wednesday evening. He tapped his finger idly against his leg while he contemplated what he had learned. There was nothing to raise any red flags. But there was also nothing indicating they had a formalized program to take in criminal defendants. *So why go out on a limb for this particular offender? It just doesn't make sense. I'm missing something. Damn it.*

He clicked on the "about" page to read up on the

pastor. He had a degree in theology from a school in Texas that Donovan had never heard of. But he wouldn't necessarily know whether the educational institution was legitimate or not. That would require a deeper dive. He put that aside for the moment. The minister's biography listed several foreign missions. *What is the connection to Miller?* Again, nothing jumped out at him. The branches of the bushes near the crawlspace rustled, and Rupert crawled out from beneath the house. Donovan closed the lid on his computer and got up to meet him.

Rupert stood up and unzipped his no-longer-white jumpsuit. He stepped out of it and threw it in his bag.

"How did it look?"

Although covered in cobwebs, Rupert did not seem concerned. He nodded in satisfaction. "No leaks. No evidence of termites. No structural subsidence."

"That's good news." Donovan's shoulders dropped as some of the tension left his body.

"Yup. I'm going to test the air conditioning and heating system now. It's fairly new. Only three years old."

"Great. I'll leave you to it. I'm going to explore the house a bit more."

While Rupert dug in his bag for his equipment, Donovan wandered down to the owner's suite. He tried to see the bedroom as Emma had envisioned it. He had very little furniture from his time in the military. *I hope Emma wants to go furniture shopping with me. No, who am I kidding? I'm buying this in the hope that Emma will make it a home. God, I hope I'm not deluding myself.* He opened the closets. There was a "his" and "hers." More than spacious enough for him. He thought back to Emma's comments. Huh. Maybe he would need to enlarge them.

He went into the master bathroom. Pulling out a notepad, he jotted down his thoughts. Remove the bathtub. He eyed the space. If he ripped out the bathtub, he could have a generous sized shower. *A shower big enough for two.* His cock twitched. He heard Rupert down the hall and started counting down backward from one hundred in increments of seven. Ninety-three. Eighty-six. The last thing he wanted was for Rupert to see him with tented pants. A loud scraping noise came from the other end of the house. Rupert was taking the grill off the front of the air conditioner to check the filter. His body was calming down. Seventy-two. Sixty-five. He continued his scrutiny of the bathroom. Fifty-eight. Fifty-one. Dual sinks. His married friends had always complained that one sink started fights. Back in the bedroom, he slid the outside door open and stepped out onto the wraparound patio. *Not great for security, but it would be nice to wake up and go right outside to see the sunrise. Better upgrade the security.*

Then he returned to the living room and picked up his tape measure. Would a pool table fit in one of the spare rooms? He busied himself measuring while Rupert moved in and out of rooms, continuing his review. When Donovan's phone pinged a text message, he pulled it out of his pocket. Emma. He quickly typed a reply.

Just then his phone rang. He winced but accepted the call.

"Hi Jack. How is everything up there?"

"Better." Satisfaction filled his voice. "Ava's dad is doing well. We'll be home in a day or so."

"I'm glad to hear that. It must be a real relief for Ava."

"It is. How is everything with Emma?"

"Well, generally fine, although it's gotten a little complicated." A shadow passed over his face.

"Complicated? How?" Jack's words were clipped. "That's generally code for problems."

Donovan explained everything that had happened in court. When he finished, Jack spewed a few inventive curse words. He held the phone away from his ear until Jack calmed down.

"Damn it. That old judge is past it. He needs to retire. But he's already announced that he'll be running for reelection." Jack paused. "I'd like to support someone to run against him."

"That would be a great idea. He needs to go. His decision didn't make any sense whatsoever."

"Yeah, about that. As a former JAG attorney, you would make a great judge."

Donovan burst out laughing. "You have got to be kidding me. And what about the job you offered me?"

"You can laugh. But I'm serious. Think about it. Of course my job offer stays open. But imagine. A former high school football star. A hometown boy made good. People eat that stuff up. Emma and I could run your campaign."

"I don't know, Jack. That's kind of a big deal. Isn't there anyone else local who might challenge the judge's reelection?"

"Well, he ran unopposed last time. Of course, his poor decisions are becoming more frequent and obvious. But the attorneys in the community aren't that ambitious. It's a great idea. Talk it over with Emma.

See what she thinks."

"I will. She's at a continuing education class today. Rupert is checking out the beach house that I put an offer in on."

"Emma told me." Jack's voice burst with enthusiasm. "It's a great location. If you fix it up, you'll increase the value exponentially. In my opinion, it's a terrific investment."

"I have to admit that I'm pretty excited. Maybe I'll give up practicing law and take up surfing. It would be a very short commute to the ocean."

Jack chuckled. "I'd pay money to see that, my overachieving friend."

The clanking of tools rang out in the background. "It sounds like Rupert is done, so I'd better go. I'm anxious to hear his preliminary report. I'll be in touch as soon as I have any news."

Rupert came back into the house, and Donovan hung up.

"Well, what do you think?" He stood with his hands on his hips and gestured with one arm. "Is the house a good buy?"

"The house looks solid." Rupert brushed dust off his clothes, then busied himself organizing his tools. "The city roof permit shows it was replaced just three years ago, at the same time as the HVAC. The plumbing is fine. Overall, the structure is sound. I found a few minor things which I'll write up in my report. I should have it to you later today. But if it were me, I would buy this house."

"That's great to hear. I've been hoping for a good report." Donovan grinned, his chest easing.

"I'll just pack up my things and head out. Tell

Emma I said hello and that I was sorry to hear about what happened to her."

"I will. She's doing well, all things considered."

"I'm glad to hear it." Rupert picked up his toolbox and headed to the front door.

Chapter 19

Emma shivered in the back of the lecture hall as a steady blast of frigid air streamed from the air conditioning vent directly above her. *Figures. And no empty seats.* She put on the cardigan that she had brought with her. *These seminars are always unbearably hot or freezing. At least I'm near the exit. I won't have to fight the masses as they rush to the women's restroom at break time.*

Bored, she doodled on her notepad. *Huh.* A house with two stick figures. A dog. *Definitely not a Freudian issue.* She flipped the page to her notes from the marketing lecture. A list of renovation ideas for Donovan's home. She pulled a face and turned to her notes from the ethics lecture. Liar. Snake. Charlatan. Her mouth tilted up. Comments about the ethics teacher, one of the most unscrupulous realtors on the island. Nothing about the actual lecture. Her thoughts shifted to Jack and Ava. She sighed loudly.

"Shush..." The woman beside her shot her a disapproving look as she hung on to the words of the lecturer and diligently took notes. Emma gritted her teeth and turned back to the presenter.

The speaker stopped for a ten-minute break to let them stretch their legs. She made her way to the refreshment station.

"Emma!" A middle-aged man, tall with thinning

hair on top hurried toward her. His loose trousers and untucked button-down shirt identified him as a local and hid the extra pounds he carried around his waist.

"Oh, hey, Pete." She hadn't spoken to the well-connected listing agent since her assault. On Victoria Island, people talked in terms of seven degrees of separation from Pete Magnuson, not Kevin Bacon.

"I heard what happened. I'm so glad you weren't hurt." Pete kissed her cheek.

Emma's jaw dropped. She thought about her head and neck injuries. "Uh, well, I was hurt enough."

"Yes, yes, of course." Pete shuffled his feet. "But you've recovered enough to be here."

"I was very lucky." Her jaw clenched. She forced a smile. She was being oversensitive. It had been a well-intentioned remark.

Pete's gaze flitted around the room and then back to Emma. He cleared his throat nervously. "I wasn't sure if I should mention this, with the assault and all, but I wanted to let you know that the property is off the market."

"Oh yeah? My client will be disappointed." In all honesty, she didn't think Ed was interested in the house after everything that had happened. And she certainly wouldn't advise a client to buy a house where illegal drugs had been manufactured.

"What with the assault and the police discovering a meth lab, the homeowners decided it wasn't a good idea to sell at this time. You know, wait until things die down a bit." Pete winked at her. "People can be superstitious about houses. They'll get a better price if they wait until the negative publicity is over."

"Yes, of course. I'll let my client know." She

pushed a stray curl behind her ear.

"Good." He patted her on the shoulder. "Sorry to disappoint, of course."

"No worries, Pete. I'll see you around."

Pete wandered off, and Emma topped up her drink from the coffee urn. She grimaced at the burnt smell of the brew. After adding a heaped spoon of powdered creamer, she took a sip and wrinkled her nose. Not much of an improvement. When she glanced around, no one seemed to be looking in her direction, so she emptied it into a potted plant and threw the cup away. As she made her way back to her seat, she stopped a few times to say hello to various acquaintances.

The lunch lecture and the rest of the afternoon passed quickly. Before the last module, she texted Donovan that she would be finished at four p.m. as expected. A reply came back almost instantly. An hour later, class ended, and she exited the building. Donovan's truck was parked in front, and she hurried over to him.

He got out of the vehicle and came around to the passenger side to open the door for her.

She hopped in, and he shut the door gently. Then he got in on the driver's side, leaned over, and kissed her. She didn't encourage him to deepen the kiss, but she didn't pull away either. *Yeah. She could give mixed signals with the best of them. She had better figure out what she wanted. It wasn't fair to Donovan.*

Donovan leaned back in his seat and turned to look at her. "I missed you today. How was your class?"

She skimmed past his first comment and answered his question. "Interesting at times. Not so much at others. But at least I received eight hours credit for continuing education. Do you mind if we stop by my apartment? I want to pick up a few things."

"Of course not." He turned north on Ocean Avenue instead of south.

Puzzled, she turned to look at him. "You know where I'm living now?"

"Jack has always kept me updated on what was going on with you. You live at the Sea Turtle Condos, right?"

"Yes." She paused. "Have you been keeping track of me all this time? I don't know if that is sweet or creepy. If it had been anyone other than you, I would say the latter. What else has Jack told you?"

"Oh, this and that." Donovan shifted in the driver's seat.

"Hmm...like what exactly?"

Donovan sighed. "I wasn't stalking you, if that is what you are asking. I just requested that he let me know if you ever started dating anyone seriously."

"And did he?"

"From time to time. I think Jack has always known how I felt about you. And that I was just waiting for the right time to make my move."

Emma looked away and didn't say anything.

His pulse quickened. "Uh, I hope that isn't a bad thing."

She tilted her head. "Honestly, I don't know. I have a lot of history to reprocess. I spent so many years thinking you thought I was a pest. Your best friend's little sister who had the hots for you. Now I find out that you liked me the whole time. Romantically, I mean. It's just a lot to take in. It's a complete turnaround, at least in my mind. And frankly, that makes me nervous. Is it for real? Will you change your mind again?" She fiddled with the bracelet on her left wrist.

He lifted her hand to his lips. "You're overthinking this. It is what it is. Two adults who like and are attracted to each other and have decided to act on that."

"Yeah, it sounds so simple when you say it that way. Why on earth didn't I think of that?"

He pulled into her condo development and parked by the entrance. She opened her door but hesitated. "Do you want to come up?"

"Sure. I'd love to see where you live." He wasn't going to let this opportunity to learn more about Emma pass by.

They skirted around a large fountain in front of the main doors. Water spewed from the mouth of an oversized fish and cascaded into the surrounding reservoir. Droplets from the spray cooled them as they entered the building. An internal staircase from the main lobby gave access to the upper floors. She led the way to 2D. Pulling her keys out of her bag, she opened the door and set her purse next to a driftwood sculpture on the entryway table. A bowl of shells sat on the low sofa table, one of several coastal accents.

Donovan looked around with interest. "I'm curious why you live in a condo. Why not buy a house as an investment? I thought that's what all realtors did."

"Now you sound like Jack. He's always on me to build up equity. But I just couldn't. Houses come with a lot of maintenance requirements. I didn't want to spend my time looking after a house and yard."

"Hey, no worries. There is no right or wrong answer. I was just curious."

She waved at the rattan love seat. "Make yourself comfortable. I'll be right back. I just want to get some more clothes." She wandered down the short hall to her bedroom. Donovan lowered himself gingerly onto her cane sofa. When it didn't creak under his weight, he sat back, rearranging the blue throw pillows behind him. Curious, he picked up one of her realtor magazines from the table and flipped through it. Slick, polished advertisements of realtors and their listings filled the marketing magazine. He shut the glossy publication. *Nothing to see here.* Emma came back carrying a small bag.

He looked up at her. "All set?"

"Yes. I hope I didn't take too long."

He shook his head. "Not at all. Here, let me take that for you." He took her duffel and with a hand low on her back guided her out of the condo.

"How about dinner? Do you want to eat out?" *A meal out was basically the definition of a date. Yeah, he could strategize with the best of them.*

"Sure. But we better stop at Jack's to let Zeus out."

"I let him out before I came to pick you up. He should be fine for a couple more hours. Where would you like to eat?"

"Do you like Mexican?"

His mouth tilted up at the corners. "Is there anyone who doesn't?"

She laughed. "Perfect. There is a great family run restaurant at the corner of First and Main streets. It's not much to look at in terms of décor, but the food is amazing."

"On it." He swung the truck around in a U-turn and headed downtown.

Emma's phone pinged. Pulling it out of her handbag, she opened her text messages.

"It's from Matt." A burst of joy warmed her heart. "He's driving back from Miami. He should be home tomorrow."

"Why was he there? Isn't the beach here nice enough? Or is it the nightlife in the city that interests him?"

Emma laughed. "Yes, to answer your unasked question. My brother's still a player. But in this case, he was taking a class to get his real estate broker's license. He's been running the rental division of Rutledge Properties, but he's getting ambitious. And yes, there are courses locally, so I suspect it was the club scene that appealed to him."

Donovan snorted. "I look forward to seeing him again. Maybe I can get a pickup game of basketball with him. I could use some exercise. And he can catch me up on what has been going on in his life."

"What? Jack didn't keep you updated on what he's been up to?"

He gave her a side glance. "No, following one of you was more than enough," Donovan said drily.

Chapter 20

With both hands wrapped around the glass, Emma slurped the last of her frozen margarita. She carefully set the massive wide-rimmed tumbler down.

"You know something? You almost waited too damn long." She accentuated her comment by pointing a tortilla chip at Donovan.

"You weren't seriously involved with that banker." He took a swig of his beer. When he set it down, beer spilled over the top.

"I could have been. Stephen and I had a lot in common."

"Yeah? Like what?"

"We both volunteered for the Save the Seas charity." She ticked one item on her finger.

"Hmm…" His eyes narrowed. "What else?"

Emma screwed her face up. She was having trouble organizing her thoughts, and this interrogation was making her think too hard. She blinked.

"He's attractive. He's my age." She counted off two more fingers. She extended another finger, then hesitated. "Oh, yes! He has a good job. That's four reasons."

He shook his head. "Those are superficial rationales at best. They don't establish long term compatibility. Anything else?"

"Uh, he was a good dancer." She made a "voila"

motion with her hands.

"Right." He set his beer down precisely on the mat. "It's clear to me that you could never have been deeply committed to him." The muscles in his shoulders relaxed.

Her face heated and she spluttered. "And wh-what makes you such an expert on me and what I need?"

Donovan grinned at her. He reached across the table and took her margarita. "They heard you across the restaurant. You're cut off from any more drinks. But to answer your question, you and I have a lot in common."

She winced. Her hand wavered as she scooped up salsa onto her tortilla chip. "Such as?"

"We share the same core values." Now he ticked items off on his fingers. "Respect, trust, loyalty, and commitment are important to us both. You care about people and animals equally. You stop your car to help a tortoise cross the road. All those care packages Jack's housekeeper sent me through the years? No matter where I was stationed? I know that it was really you who put them together. That's kindness. We have shared interests, such as working out. Whenever we're together, we have fun. Oh, and our chemistry is off the charts. Can you say any of that about Stephen?"

She wiped up the salsa that had fallen off her chip and onto the tablecloth. Finally she looked up.

"No, I can't say that." Her shoulders hunched.

"Was anything I said incorrect?"

"No." Her chin dropped.

"Are you done playing with your food?"

She sighed. "Yes."

He signaled to the waiter. "Can we have the check

please?"

"Of course, sir. I'll be right back."

The waiter returned promptly with the bill, and Donovan took care of payment. "Have a good evening, folks.

"You, too."

Donovan pulled out Emma's chair. She wobbled on her high-heeled sandals, and he held her steady. "Easy now."

"I think that margarita hit me a bit harder than I thought." She laughed self-consciously. He wrapped his arm around her waist and held her steady as she walked.

"You think? Did you eat any lunch?"

She scrunched her face as she thought. "No, not much. There wasn't much for a vegetarian on the catered lunch the course provided."

"See? Just an example of you caring for animals and for your health."

She giggled. "You're determined to make your case."

"Yes, I am. Is it working?" Donovan inhaled her jasmine scent.

She gave him a coy look. "Wouldn't you like to know?"

He shook his head and stabilized her as they walked to his truck. He opened the passenger door and lifted her onto the seat. She couldn't repress a giggle.

"My he-man," she said, squeezing his bicep.

"Whatever," he mumbled.

"Did you say something?"

"No."

He got into the driver seat. She fumbled with the

clasp on her seat belt, so he leaned over and fastened it for her. Then he started the engine, put the truck in drive, and headed south on Victoria Parkway. The dashboard lights glowed as the automatic headlights turned on. Several minutes passed without seeing another vehicle.

He glanced in the rearview mirror as a car came up behind them with its high beams on. "Damn it."

Emma caught some of the reflection in the mirror. "Those lights are bright."

"Hang on tight. We have trouble." He accelerated, and Emma braced a hand on the dashboard. He cursed as the sedan closed the gap. The truck juddered forward when the car hit the back of his bumper. Their heads flew back and hit the headrests.

Emma smothered a scream. The truck fishtailed, and he corrected the steering, so it stayed straight. He sped up, but the driver behind stepped on the gas too.

"Call 911." Sweat beaded on his forehead. He grasped the steering wheel so tightly it was as if his hands were welded to it. It took all his concentration to keep the truck on the road.

She fumbled for her cell phone and hit the emergency number. The police dispatcher picked up. The car hit them again, and she shouted into the phone. "We need help. We're heading south on Victoria Parkway, and a car is ramming us." Her voice, a few octaves higher than normal, cracked.

"What?" She pulled the phone away from her ear. "They say to go to the nearest police station."

He uttered an expletive. "Tell them to send a fucking police car."

There was a sharp crack and a splintering sound.

Emma wailed, and Donovan took one hand off the wheel and pushed her head down. A small hole perforated the back window. Spiderweb cracks radiated out from the void like bicycle spokes.

"They're shooting at us." Emma yelled into the phone, raw panic in her voice.

Another blast, and the window fractured. Donovan twisted the wheel back and forth, weaving the truck. "Stay down and hang on. I'm trying to make it difficult for them to hit us."

Emma's hand shook as she held the phone. "They're sending help."

"About damn time. Hang on. I don't want to be run off the road where we'll be sitting ducks. There's no way to do a U-turn here. Better to take control of the situation. I'm going to slam on the brakes. He'll hit us, but we should be okay. Hopefully our airbags won't deploy if we're hit from behind, but theirs will. They'll be trapped."

"All right." The hammering in her chest intensified. The phone slid through her sweaty hands and fell onto the floorboard.

"Here we go." He slammed on the brakes. The vehicle behind hit the back of his truck, jolting them forward and then slinging them back.

"Emma! Emma! Talk to me! Where does it hurt?" He didn't see any blood, but she was too still. *Had he miscalculated the whiplash she would suffer?*

After a beat Emma laughed shakily and gasped. "I'm fine. I just need to get my breath back."

"Stay here. Keep your head down."

"There's no chance of me moving." She flinched when she shifted slightly and jarred her neck.

He reached below his seat and pulled out a gun. Releasing the lock, he opened the door and slipped out. *Thank God I disabled the interior light.* He hunched over and ran to the car behind. The impact of the crash had crumpled the gunmetal gray sedan and wedged it under the bed of his truck. Both occupants were pinned by the airbags. The driver groaned as he lay slumped. Donovan put his fingers on his neck. *Good. A strong pulse.* The unconscious passenger leaned against the door of the car. His chest rose and fell in a steady rhythm.

He pulled his cell phone out of his pocket and dialed 911 to update the dispatcher.

A few minutes later, but which seemed like an eternity, the siren of the police car blared as it approached. The ambulance followed. Mike got out of the patrol car.

"Two badly injured here. I think you'll need the Jaws of Life to extract them," Donovan reported.

Mike looked over at the car and its inhabitants. He reached up to his radio and called for the fire truck. The paramedics ran over to them.

"The fire department is on the way. They're five minutes out," Mike said.

One of the EMTs poked his head in the window. "Good. These guys are going to need it. You in the front vehicle?"

"Yes."

"Any pain?"

"No. But could you check on my girlfriend? She's still in the truck. She says she's fine, but I'd appreciate if you checked her out."

The medic trotted off to the passenger side of the

truck. He opened the door and leaned in. Emma rocked gently, huddled in on herself.

"Are you hurt, ma'am?"

"No. Just shaken up." She wiped her eyes. *God, don't let me cry again.*

"What happened to the back window?" He glanced curiously at the splintered glass. "That wasn't caused by a collision."

Emma stammered her response. "They s-s-shot it out."

He whistled and shook his head. "Damn. You were lucky. If you start to feel any pain, give me a shout. I better get back to the guys in the car."

She grabbed his arm. "Be careful. They have a gun."

"I will." After glancing back at the crumpled car, the paramedic responded, "But I don't think those guys are in a position to do any more harm. At least not at the moment."

A fire truck wailed as it ground to a halt behind the entwined vehicles, and a pair of muscled firefighters jumped out. They surveyed the car and in concert turned to pull equipment from the ladder truck.

"Come on, Donovan. Let's get out of the way and let them get to work with the Jaws of Life."

Mike set up flood lights. His partner directed the infrequent traffic around the accident area, shouting to be heard over the noise of the generator powering the fireman's tools. One of the rescuers picked up the spreader and pushed it into the gap where the car door closed. The hydraulics hissed as he slowly pried the door open. The paramedic leaned in to check the driver while the fireman jogged around the car and started the process to extract the passenger.

Mike turned to Donovan. "Good. They're making progress getting them out. I wanted to tell you that I've been keeping Ken up to date with what has been happening here."

Donovan raised an eyebrow. "Not a fan of the acting chief?"

"Rawlings?" Mike snorted. "Chief was pressured by one of the city commissioners to hire him as deputy."

"Smalltown life."

"No kidding. But anyway, Ken is coming down for the weekend to look into these incidents. It's a black mark on his policing, and he's not happy about it. He's a good friend of Jack's, so I'm sure he'll be in touch with you."

"I would appreciate that. I get the feeling Acting Chief Rawlings isn't a storming intellect."

"Understatement of the year." Mike commented without inflection.

One of the paramedics bent over the driver as he lay on a gurney "He's got a pulse. Get an oxygen mask on him and transport him. I'll stay with the passenger." His partner nodded.

"When they get the passenger out, search for a gun. Those bastards shot at us. They should be charged with attempted murder."

Mike raised an eyebrow.

Donovan held up his hands. "Sorry, I didn't mean to tell you how to do your job."

Mike waved his apology off. "No problem. You and Emma have certainly pissed someone off. Don't worry. As soon as they finish I'll look for their weapons. Let me see what their prognosis is. I'll need to talk to them at the hospital if at all possible. I'll also have to get your statement and Emma's as well."

"No problem. We can head to the police station."

"Hang on just a minute." Mike hurried over to the second paramedic. "How are they?"

His lined face and matter-of-fact expression evidenced his long experience. "Hard to say. They're both unconscious and will likely need surgery."

"I guess I won't be talking to them anytime soon."

"No. Definitely not."

"Thanks, man." He walked back to Donovan.

"I'll get a tow truck for both vehicles. I won't be able to interview either of them for a while."

"Can you give us a ride to Jack's? I can pick up Emma's car, and we'll meet you at the police station."

"Of course. I'd say you could come in tomorrow, but I had better interview you tonight since those two aren't in great shape. Best to get your version of events on the record."

"No problem. I'll just get Emma."

He walked back to his truck and leaned in the passenger side.

"How are you doing, kitten?" he asked gently.

Emma looked blankly at him. "I'm fine."

He reached in and cupped her cheek with his hand. "You're doing great. But I need you to hang in there a little longer. Mike's going to take us to pick up your car, then we need to go to the station to make statements. Do you think you're up to that?"

"Of course." She swallowed the lump in her throat.

"Good girl." He carefully helped her get down from the truck.

Chapter 21

Emma put her head on the table. "My goodness. What time is it? How long will we need to stay here?" Her eyelids shut involuntarily, and she jerked them open. "Oh my God! We won't be charged with anything, will we?"

Donovan rubbed her back and glanced at his watch. One a.m.

"We haven't done anything wrong, kitten. It's not a crime to defend yourself when you're being shot at. I'll go check with Mike. We've both written our statements. I don't see any reason why we need to be here any longer." As he got up, the door to the interview room opened, and Chief Rawlings swaggered in.

"Please sit down. Can I get you anything?"

"No, thanks, Chief. You have our accounts." He pushed the handwritten statements across the table. "It's late and time for us to go."

"Well now, I just have a few more questions." He turned on the recorder and stated their names and the time.

Donovan shook his head wearily. "Chief, Emma and I are done in. We've been in a car accident. This is the second time in a week that Emma's suffered an injury. She hasn't had any medical attention. I need to get her home."

"Did you actually see a gun pointed at your truck?"

"Are you kidding me, Chief?" Blood boiling, he fought the urge to jump across the table and throttle Rawlings. He gritted his teeth and bit out his response. "I've been in the military deployed in hot zones for fifteen years. I know the sound of a gun firing. Have your officers done a forensic search of my vehicle? They'll find the bullets. I sure as hell didn't shoot out the back window of my truck. Now, since we're not under arrest, I'm going to take Emma and get her medically checked out. Then we're going home to sleep."

Rawlings waved his arm dismissively. "Now, Donovan, no need to get defensive. We just need to clear up a few things."

"No, we don't. There's nothing to resolve." Donovan pulled out Emma's chair and escorted her out of the interview room, slamming the door behind him. Mike swiveled his chair away from his desk and gestured imperceptibly to the restroom.

Donovan put his hands on her shoulders. "Wait for me in reception? I'll be right out. I won't be long. I promise. I just need you to bear with me a little while longer. And if Chief Rawlings approaches you, just smile and say you have nothing to add."

Emma struggled to keep her eyes open. She walked out to the waiting area, taking a seat on the bench. But before long, she leaned over and curled up, making herself as small as possible.

Donovan headed into the men's restroom. A minute later, the door opened, and Mike came in. He turned on the faucet for some background noise.

"Can you make sure they search my truck for the

bullet that went in the window? You should also find one somewhere on the tailgate. I don't like the direction Rawlings is headed. I'm not convinced he'll use due diligence."

A muscle in Mike's face twitched. "Yeah, sure, the guy who does forensics is a buddy of mine. I'm sure he would do that anyway no matter what Chief Rawlings says. He's a good officer. And Rawlings isn't a popular guy here."

"Well, I'm not as convinced. The chief was just trying to interrogate us about whether we saw a gun. I don't trust that guy."

"I don't disagree with you there. I'll get right on it. Get some sleep. I'll call you in the morning."

"Thanks."

"Anytime."

Donovan exited the restroom. Mike waited a minute before leaving.

When Donovan got to the lobby, Emma lay lengthwise on the bench with her back to the room. "Emma, time to go." She snored softly. "Looks like you're already away with the fairies." He picked her up. Whoosh. She stirred when the automatic door to the police station opened, but she didn't wake up. He reached into his pocket to unlock the SUV and opened the door. She roused as he lifted her in and put her in the passenger seat.

"Are we going home now?" she mumbled.

"Shh...go back to sleep." He leaned in and fastened her seat belt. He shut the door quietly and walked around to the driver side, slid in, and closed the door. Buckling up, he started the car and headed home. Funny how quickly Jack's house had become his temporary home. He kept within the speed limit as he drove and signaled each turn. *It would be just like that bastard to have me pulled over for a traffic violation.* In ten minutes, they were pulling into Jack's driveway. He tapped Emma's garage door opener and after pulling into the garage, he looked around before shutting the garage door and getting out of the SUV. He lifted Emma out. She wrapped her arms around his neck and tucked her head against his shoulder.

"I'm glad we're home," she murmured. "Let's go to bed."

"That's the plan, kitten." He adjusted her in his arms, so he had a firm grip on her.

Donovan carried her inside, kicking the garage door shut with his foot and turning to engage the double lock. He hefted her through the living room and up the stairs, opening the door to her bedroom. Zeus bounded up behind him as he set Emma down on the bed.

"I'm going to let Zeus out for a bathroom break. Can you get ready for bed?"

"Of course. I'm not a child."

He let her comment pass. She was understandably upset. It had been a hell of an evening.

Retracing his steps to the garage, he retrieved his gun from the glove box. Then he returned to the living room where Zeus waited. "Come on, Zeus, you're with me." Zeus trotted behind him. He didn't turn on the patio lights and waited while Zeus peed on one of Ava's large potted plants and came trotting back to the house.

"Good boy." He hoped Ava would forgive him for the positive reinforcement. He patted Zeus on the head and re-locked the door.

"Go to bed, Zeus." Zeus disappeared in the direction of the laundry room where he had one of his many dog beds. Donovan went back upstairs to check on Emma. Her door was open. She lay on her side in bed but had a side light on. She reached out to him.

"Come to bed with me, Donovan. We've waited long enough." Her voice quivered. "We could have been killed tonight." He sat down next to her and kissed her on the forehead. "I don't want to spend the rest of my life angry at you," she whispered. "I don't want to miss out on life because I'm afraid to take a chance. Afraid to trust."

He shook his head and cleared his throat. "Not that I'm objecting. In fact, there is nothing I would like more. But you're half asleep. And you've had a traumatic experience. I don't want our first time to be about burning adrenaline. When we finally get together, it will be special. I'll share your bed, but we should sleep. And that's all. I'll be right back." He stood and yanked his shirt over his head exposing his six pack abs and hair which tapered to a "V" just above his jeans

She watched him with eyelids half closed. Despite her exhaustion, her pulse raced. He didn't get those muscles from sitting at a desk all day.

Unzipping his jeans, he stepped out of them and tossed them on the chair. Then he lifted the covers and crawled into bed wearing just his boxers. He pulled her back against his chest, spooning her. He inhaled her scent, reveling in the closeness before kissing her on the neck. "Sleep, little kitten."

"Goodnight, Donovan." She snuggled back against him, and he smothered a groan as her backside came into contact with his groin. After a few minutes he rolled onto his back and stared at the ceiling. He was awake a long time thinking about the events of the day.

Chapter 22

Zeus nudged his arm with a cool moist nose. Donovan squinted at the early morning sunlight and groaned. "I bet you have to go out, don't you, Zeus?"

A high-pitched whine urged him on.

He threw the covers back. "I'm coming. Hold your horses."

"What's going on?" Emma stirred and mumbled, half asleep.

"No need to get up yet. I'm just going to let Zeus out. I'll be right back." He slid out of bed and opened the bedroom door. Zeus followed him close on his heels. They hurried down the stairs and headed to the back door.

"Come on, Zeus. Be quick about it." Donovan turned the alarm off. Zeus dashed out the door and scampered straight to his favorite potted plant before returning to the house.

"Good boy."

After reengaging the security, Donovan pointed to the laundry room. "Go to your bed."

Zeus whimpered.

"No excuses. Bed."

His head hanging low, Zeus padded off to his lair off the kitchen.

Donovan ran up the stairs two at a time. Emma rolled over when he entered the room. He climbed into bed and pulled her into his arms.

"I was wondering if you meant what you said last night?" His hand fondled the curve of her hip.

Flustered, she racked her brains for what to say. In the end, stalling seemed the best option. "I said many things."

"You told me you were ready to move forward with our relationship."

"Oh, that." Her cheeks burned. "Yes. I did say that."

When she didn't elaborate, Donovan continued. "And did you mean it?"

"Yes," she said quietly. Swallowing, she paused a beat. Yes, I did."

Donovan exhaled loudly. "Thank God. That was all I needed to hear." He found her mouth with a drugging kiss. She closed her eyes as a myriad of emotions engulfed her. Incredulity. Disbelief. Wonder. Then she could no longer think as a wave of euphoria overwhelmed her and she wrapped her arms around his shoulders, pulling him in closer. She ran a finger lightly up his washboard abs. "I like this," she murmured.

"All yours," he whispered as he slid down her body raining kisses as he went. His hand inched up under the college T-shirt she slept in and toyed with her nipple. Warmth flooded her core. He pulled her shirt over her head and dropped it over the edge of the bed. His eyes heated and he sucked in a breath as she lay there in only her black lace thong.

"Beautiful." He leaned down and kissed her flat stomach, following with a line of kisses down to her core. She jerked.

"Don't," she murmured then jerked when his

mouth hit a sensitive spot and a spark of electricity shot through her.

"Don't what?

"Don't stop."

"I won't, kitten." He laughed. "We'll be so good together." He pulled down her underwear and her breath quickened. "Oh my God." Disjointed thoughts rushed through her mind, disorienting her. Intense pleasure. So good. Could this really be Donovan? Then no thoughts at all. Only feeling.

Putting his mouth on her center, he tugged on her with first his mouth and then his fingers, and the pressure built to a crescendo.

He tweaked her once again, and bright lights obscured her vision. She exploded in a thousand pieces. After, her muscles languid, she struggled to focus. Before she fully recovered, Donovan took off his briefs. He fumbled in the pocket of his jeans for a condom and ripped the packet open with his teeth. Rolling it on, he moved over her. The bed creaked in a steady rhythm. A coiling pressure, until finally a flash bang and her world shattered again.

"So much better than I imagined." He kissed her gently.

"That was amazing." Her skin prickled as the cool air hit her, and she pulled the silky white sheet up. When her breathing eased, she laughed. "I hate to say this but you were right."

"Oh yeah?" Propped on one elbow, he smoothed her sweaty hair back. "What about?"

"Us. It's always been you. I wish we'd gotten together before. We wasted so much time."

"Hey. We both needed that experience to bring us

to this point." He pulled her in and wrapped his arms around her. "It had to be this way. But we're here now. Let's make the most of our future together."

She smiled. "Works for me."

Something crashed to the floor downstairs followed by a curse. Donovan jumped out of the bed. "Stay here. Lock the door behind me."

He pulled his jeans on quickly and took his gun out of the bedside table where he had put it the night before. Slipping out the bedroom door, he held the gun pointed at the ground and crept down the stairs. At the bottom, he stopped and listened. The clink of dishes came from the kitchen. He peeked around the corner. Matt rummaged in a kitchen cabinet. Donovan put the gun on the table.

"Hey, Matt! Good to see you, man."

Matt whirled around. A younger version of Jack stared at him. The same brown hair, intense blue eyes, and angular face

"Donovan, great to have you home!" Donovan bumped fists and then gave Matt a quick man hug and a thump on the back.

Just then Emma came into the kitchen wearing her shorts and a T-shirt. Her damp hair hung in ringlets around her face. "I heard your voice." She threw her arms around Matt and gave him a hug.

"It's so good to have you home! You won't believe what's been going on." She filled him in.

"What. The. Fuck. That's absolutely crazy. Are you okay? Does Jack know about this?"" He raked his fingers through his hair.

"Yes, yes, we're both fine. And Jack knows everything. Donovan has been taking good care of me."

Matt looked from Emma to Donovan, and then back at her. Matt raised his eyebrow at Donovan. "Finally?"

Donovan laughed. "Yes, I made my move."

"Damn. Jack won the bet." He put his hands over his face and shook his head in mock despair.

"Hey!" Emma put her hands on her hips. "You and Jack bet on whether I would get together with Donovan?"

Matt laughed. "You have to admit, sis, it's been a long time coming."

She looked pointedly at Donovan. "Huh! I'm not the one who took so long making up his mind."

"Timing is everything." His eyes crinkled at the corners. "I had better go get dressed.

A few minutes later, Donovan came downstairs, whistling for Zeus. "I'll let Zeus out and be right back. "Come on, buddy." He opened the door, and Zeus christened the same planter. *Better break that habit before Ava returns.* After letting him back in, he returned to the kitchen and found Emma grinding beans. Matt sat at the table.

Emma looked up at Donovan. "How do you want your coffee?"

"Black, please." He sat on one of the bar stools at the kitchen island. Emma handed him a mug.

"Matt, here's the creamer. I know you'll want it." Emma slid the pot across the island to Matt along with his mug of coffee. She poured one for herself and then sat opposite them.

"Thanks, sis." He turned to Donovan. "While you were in the shower, Jack called. Everything is going to hit the fan. He was going to call Ken as soon as he hung up with me."

"I suspect Ken was already on it. I spoke with Mike last night, and he said Ken was returning to supervise things."

"Well, let's put this aside for a few minutes. An army marches on its stomach. We need to eat first. How about omelets and toast?" Emma interjected. It wouldn't hurt to try to get a little normality back into their lives.

"Sounds great." Donovan raised his cup for a sip.

"Works for me. Donovan, could I talk to you for a minute?" Matt looked at him purposefully.

"Of course."

Matt gestured to the door. "Let's go out to the patio."

"Oh, come on, guys." Emma crossed her arms over her chest. "I'm not a child, you know. Whatever you want to say, Matt, you can say in front of me."

"I know, sis. But we'll be right back." Matt signaled to Donovan to follow him. Donovan closed the door behind him.

They sat in chairs by the pool. Matt leaned forward, his elbows on his knees. "Now tell me what's *really* going on."

"Hell if I know." Donovan rubbed the back of his neck. "But it's got to be related to Emma's assault. She saw something that is dangerous for someone, only she doesn't know what it is."

"Jack is going to add the full force of his weight to the investigation. Frankly, I'm surprised he waited so long to light a fire under Ken Davidson."

Donovan ran his hand through his short hair. "I'd be a fool to say 'no' to that given Emma's safety is at stake."

"Sounds fine. Come on. I'm starving. Let's go eat."
Donovan and Matt headed back into the house.

Chapter 23

Emma's phone rang while they were eating, and Emma looked at the screen.

"Unknown caller."

"Let me answer. Just in case." Donovan held out his hand for her phone. Emma glanced again at the screen but then reluctantly handed it over to him. Her throat closed up. She hated having to take these extra precautions. Donovan hit the accept button.

"Yeah?"

"This is Chief Rawlings. I'm calling for Emma."

"Chief, this is Donovan Evans. I'm also her attorney. How can I help?"

"Well, I wanted to speak to you too, so I'm glad I have you on the phone. I'd like you both to come down to the station to answer some additional questions."

"I don't know what other information you could need from us. In any event, I'm afraid I have to decline your invitation on behalf of both of us. We're suffering the aftereffects of the car accident."

Matt raised an eyebrow. Donovan shrugged.

"I thought you would want to help the investigation, not impede it."

"Enough. My patience with you has run out. The only one hindering the investigation is you. There is absolutely no point in Emma and me coming to the station."

"That's outrageous." Rawlings' voice shook. "I demand that you both come in."

"That's not going to happen, Chief. If you have any sensible questions, I'd be prepared to consider them once we've recovered from the accident. Goodbye." Donovan hit the end button.

Matt chuckled. "That's going to cause a stir down at the police station."

"Let it. I didn't like where the interview was going last night. It should all be pretty straightforward. They should have the forensics by now, which will show the bullets that hit my truck. And they must have found the gun in the car that hit us. The bastards wouldn't have been able to ditch it after the accident. They were both out of it."

Emma's phone pinged with a text. "Harry's here."

Donovan frowned "Harry?"

She made a face. "Yes, Harry. He's Jack's handyman. He's worked for him for years—he's not a threat."

Donovan glanced at Matt, who added, "We've known Harry forever."

"I'll let him in through the garage." She went down the hall.

Emma's phone rang again. Donovan picked it up and answered.

"This is Ken Davidson. I'm Victoria City's chief of police. I'm calling for Emma Rutledge."

"Chief Davidson, this is Donovan Evans. I'm Emma's attorney."

"Hello, Donovan. Jack told me about you. Call me Ken. I'm flying down from Quantico and should be there this afternoon to find out what's going on. I'd like to meet with you and Emma this afternoon if that would be convenient."

"That can be arranged. Where and when do you want to get together?"

"I'm going into the station to review the evidence. How about I see you at Jack's house around three p.m.?"

"We'll see you then, Chief." He hung up and set the phone down. "I do believe Jack has pulled some strings. Chief Davidson will be here this afternoon. Let's see what he has to say."

"Jack and Ken have known each other a long time. This should be interesting." Matt stirred his coffee. "Ken should be able to straighten out Rawlings."

Emma walked back into the kitchen with an older man.

"Donovan, meet Harry. He's Jack's super-handyman. There isn't much he can't fix."

Harry's chest puffed out in his denim coveralls. He took off his baseball cap and twisted it in his hands.

Emma picked up the pot. "How do you take your coffee?"

"Black, please." She handed him a fresh mug.

"Thanks. I'll just raise the hurricane shutters so Bob can bring in the replacement windows."

"That's fine. When he does, send him to the kitchen for coffee."

Harry put his baseball cap back on.

"All right. Harry has everything he needs. Ed wants me to find some more houses for him to view, so I should spend the morning looking at the listings online."

Donovan looked at Matt. "How about a game of

pool?"

"You're on. I wouldn't mind taking some more money off you." Matt rubbed his hands together. They went down the hallway to the game room where Jack had a full-size pool table. After racking the balls, Matt gestured to Donovan. "You break. Age before beauty."

"Huh…watch and learn, grasshopper." Donovan landed a solid ball in the pocket. He proceeded to clear the table of several more balls until he missed a shot.

"Aha. My turn." Matt chalked his cue and sunk a striped ball in the side pocket just as Emma wandered in.

"Hey, guys, I've found a few more properties for Ed to view." She surveyed the pool table which had only a few balls remaining on it. "Who's winning?"

"Donovan at this point." Matt tapped his fingers on the edge of the pool table. "But not for long."

Emma sat on the sofa. "When you're finished beating your chests to see who the bigger man is, I'll show you the properties I found. But I can see that this game may take a while." She settled down to watch as they continued to play.

Chapter 24

Later that afternoon, a nondescript four-door sedan pulled into the driveway. A tall, lean man wearing a baseball hat got out. A car door slammed shut.

Donovan glanced out the window. "If that's Ken, he's early."

Emma leaned around him and peered out the window. "Yes, that's him."

Donovan opened the door.

Emma pushed past Donovan to hug Ken. "How are you? Come inside."

"Hello Emma, it's good to see you. And to see that you're okay."

"I appreciate you coming back. Ken, I want you to meet Donovan Evans. He's an old friend of the family."

Donovan extended his hand, and Ken gripped it firmly. "I'm sorry for what's happened to you both, and for Rawlings. I'll set him straight."

"I'd appreciate that. The more time he wastes looking into us, the less resources and time he'll have to put into a proper investigation."

Ken took off his hat and set it on the table in the entryway before following them into the living room. He took a seat, and Emma handed him a steaming mug. Smiling gratefully, he sipped, then set it on the table. He leaned forward and clasped his hands together. "Thanks for seeing me today."

"Of course. We want to help any way we can. Other than timewasting activities, that is."

Ken cleared his throat. "Well, this is a delicate matter. But Jack and I have been friends a long time, and I want to make sure that no harm comes to Emma."

"We appreciate that." Donovan put his arm around Emma's shoulder and pulled her into his side.

"I'm going to personally oversee the police inquiry even when I'm back in Virginia. Mike has been keeping me updated with what's been going on. First, I can tell you that forensics found the bullet holes in your truck and the gun in the car that hit you. They match. So there is no doubt that you were fired on with a deadly weapon. I read your statements. They are consistent with the forensics. Unfortunately, we can't question either of the men in the car yet for medical reasons. But I should make it clear that no further interrogation of either of you is necessary. I do not foresee charging you with any crime."

Donovan quirked an eyebrow. "I didn't think so. But I certainly appreciate you confirming it."

Ken leaned back against the sofa. "I would like to hear your thoughts about these incidents and how they might relate."

Donovan filled him in on what he had pieced together, which wasn't much.

"I'll have Mike investigate the church and its pastor. Here's my business card with my direct cell number. Don't hesitate to use it at any time." Ken handed his card to Donovan.

"I'll walk you out." Donovan gestured for Ken to precede him to the door.

Ken turned to Donovan. "I can't guarantee that

Emma isn't in further danger."

"I know. I'll protect her. But if you can get to the bottom of who is after her, that would be appreciated. Oh, and keep Chief Rawlings on a leash."

Ken looked up briefly before responding. "He wasn't my choice for deputy." He shook his head. "I moved here to get away from the violence in the big city. Which pretty much up until this case I did. But it's smalltown politics. Parochial life. It requires some compromises. I'm learning as I go."

"I understand."

Ken shook Donovan's hand. "I'll be in touch." He got into his vehicle and drove away.

Donovan returned to the house just as Matt was preparing to leave.

"Are you heading out, Matt?"

"Yeah, I've got to go home too." He tossed his car keys in the air. "I'll be in the office tomorrow. But call me if you need anything. Any time of the day or night."

"We will. Thanks, Matt." Emma kissed him on the cheek.

Chapter 25

Emma returned to the living room. Donovan busied himself in the kitchen making fresh coffee. He took their mugs into the living room and sat next to Emma on the sofa. Placing them on the table, he shifted in his seat and faced her.

"Are you going to tell me what's bothering you now?" He tilted his head and raised an eyebrow.

Emma rotated her neck to ease the tension in her muscles. "What do you mean?"

He exhaled loudly. "Come on, Emma. I can tell when you're distracted or worrying. You're both now. So come clean."

"There's no hiding anything from you."

"A problem shared is a problem halved."

"I never thought you would resort to platitudes."

"It may be a cliche, but that doesn't make it any less true." He put his hand on her thigh. "Let me help you."

"Stop." She held her hands up in surrender. "You've convinced me. Those houses I showed you and Matt? The ones I found for Ed to view?" Clearing her throat, she hesitated before answering. "I'm terrified to go into a house alone. When I think of scheduling the viewings, I shake, and my heart races. I was okay taking you to house showings. But going alone? That scares the hell out of me." She spit the words out. "I hate that Miller stole my independence. I just hate that."

Donovan put his arm around her and pulled her into his side.

"Hey. Listen to me, sweetheart. That's completely normal. You've been the victim of violence. You're having a post-traumatic stress reaction."

Emma's face closed down. "But isn't that for repeated exposure? Such as war? I've only been hit on the head and choked by a criminal."

He shook his head. "Don't belittle what happened to you. And it's not just long-term combat that causes PTSD. It can be caused by an assault such as you experienced. And don't forget that Jack's house was sprayed with gunfire or the men who shot at us. We had a lot of training in the military to recognize the signs of PTSD. I've seen it in my friends. Hell, I've experienced it myself. Have you had nightmares?"

"Yes. I wake up in the middle of the night, sweating. Reliving what happened. But I thought it was the pain medication causing the nightmares."

"Emma, honey, I'm no doctor, but it sure sounds like a stress reaction to me. Sometimes the symptoms go away with time, and sometimes they don't. Either way, it's nothing to be ashamed about." He pushed her hair off her face.

"And if that's what's happening to me?" She took a deep breath. "How do I make it stop?"

"In time it may get better on its own. If it doesn't, it might help to talk to a therapist. But in the short term, focus on the here and now."

Emma wrapped her arms around herself and looked at him doubtfully. "That's easier said than done."

"I know. But just try to be fully aware of how you're feeling and what's happening in the present. So you don't dwell on the bad things that happened. I use it when I'm stressed by work. It also helps me focus under pressure. For the time being, I'm going to stick with you 24/7. You won't have to go anywhere by yourself. And if for some reason I can't go with you, Matt will go with you. You're not in this alone. Remember that." He ran his finger down her cheek. She put her hand over his hand and held his hand against her face.

"True." She pulled away. "I'll make those appointments for the homes that Ed wants to see. As long as you're with me, I know I'll be fine. But at some point, I need to be able to go into a deserted house by myself."

He put his hands on her face and looked directly into her eyes. "And you will. You'll get there. I promise you that. But a few days after you were just assaulted is *not* the time to force the issue. You need to process what's happened and heal."

She swallowed and looked away. "Well, uh, I hope you like walking through a lot of houses."

"Sure. It's not a problem. Maybe I'll get some ideas for my renovation."

"That's the spirit. Remember that as we look at yet another kitchen." She laughed. "But you'll like Ed. He fishes. A lot."

"Good. Now, about my house…"

"Now that Rupert has given it a clean bill of health, it's just the financing to arrange. Are you going to mortgage it?"

"In a manner of speaking. I'm not using a bank

though. Jack is handling the loan for me."

"That's all set then. I can recommend an architect for any remodeling you may want to do."

"That would be great." He paused and looked meaningfully at her. "I'd also like your input."

Emma leaned back on the sofa. "Sure. I'll see if I can get Juan Garcia to meet with us tomorrow after Ed's last house viewing. Juan is the architect Jack uses for a lot of his projects. He does amazing work."

Chapter 26

The next morning Emma and Donovan headed to a house on the north end of Victoria Island. Emma glanced at her watch and frowned. "We're supposed to meet Ed at ten. We're going to be a little late."

"Ed's a laidback kind of guy, isn't he? He'll wait." Donovan adjusted the driver's seat in Emma's SUV.

"I know. It's just unprofessional." Her brows drew together. "It's not like me to be late. I pride myself on giving my clients the best possible service."

Keeping one hand on the steering wheel, he brought her hand to his lips and kissed it. "I know. And Ed understands what you've been through. You're just going through some difficult times. You have to be easier on yourself."

"If you were late to court, how would you feel? My job and how I perform it is as important to me as yours is to you."

"Huh." Donovan paused. "Well, it's a moot point, because we're almost there." He turned down a side street into a neighborhood of well cared for homes that had been built in the 1950s. Donovan slowed as a couple of cyclists teetered as they slowly pedaled down the street. A "for sale" sign was planted in the grass of a rambling single-story red brick house. He pulled into the driveway and parked.

The droning of machinery from the paper mill

across the water buzzed in the background. A strong wind blew from the plant toward them, bringing with it the unpleasant smell of rotten eggs.

"Do you think the noise and smell will put Ed off?"

"I doubt it. Anyone who grew up on the island knows about the mill and the issues associated with it. I think if he likes the house, it won't matter."

Ed pulled up in his truck as Emma was getting the key out of the lockbox. Emma took a deep breath and raised a hand in greeting.

"Good girl," Donovan whispered in her ear. "You're doing great."

She squeezed his hand before greeting her client. "How are you doing, Ed?"

"I'm fine, Emma, and I sure am glad to see you looking so good." Ed hooked his thumbs in the front pocket of his plaid Bermuda shorts. He wore a T-shirt that proclaimed, "I'd rather be fishing." Ed held out his hand to Donovan.

"I'm Ed Morganfield." Sweat glistened on Ed's brow, and his face was red from the heat.

"Donovan Evans. Pleased to meet you. I'll be accompanying Emma on house viewings. I hope you don't mind."

"No problem at all. I'm glad Emma has someone looking out for her. It was a very scary incident. I'm just glad I found her so quickly."

Donovan's eyes flared. "I'm glad you were there too. Thank you for taking care of Emma."

Emma shifted her weight from one foot to the other and looked around, anywhere but at the men. *Time for a change of subject.* "Shall we get out of the sun?" Emma steered both men toward the house. As she flipped

160

through her notes, she described the house's highlights. "Ed, this is a four bedroom, two and a half bath. I selected it because it has a dock where you can moor your boat."

"Outstanding. Can't wait to see the outside." Ed rubbed his hands together gleefully.

"What about the house?"

"The house is less interesting to me than the water access." Ed paused. He swallowed deeply. "Of course, that may be why my wife left me. She always said I was obsessed with fishing."

Emma's face softened. "Come on. Let's take a look inside." To the left of the entryway, a small living area had four formal chairs surrounding a coffee table. Freshly cut white roses protruded from a crystal vase. To the right, a walnut dining room table with beautifully contoured Queen Anne legs was surrounded by four matching chairs with tapestry seat cushions. Ed gave both rooms a cursory look, then continued into the great room. A sliding glass door opened to the backyard. Ed's gaze targeted the rear garden like a heat seeking missile.

Emma's eyes lit up with amusement. "Why don't we look outside, Ed?" She opened the door. A wall of humidity slapped them in the face. The smell of the marsh which lined the intracoastal waterway overpowered them. Salt, sulfur, and the rank smell of seaweed assaulted them, overcoming any smell from the paper mill. Emma wrinkled her nose. Seemingly unbothered by the odor, Ed walked past her, scrutinizing the area. Donovan trailed behind keeping an eye on their surroundings. A long path meandered through native plants. Several citrus trees loaded with lemons and oranges provided color and shade. The path ended at a boardwalk that led to a dock suitable for a small motorboat.

"You could launch from this dock. Or just fish from the landing." Ed rubbed his hands together in delight.

"This house is under budget. It's been on and off the market a while, and the owners are anxious to sell."

"Do you know why they're selling?" Ed's gaze wandered over the property.

"They want to sell up and move near their daughter in North Carolina."

"That makes sense. I guess we should see the rest of the inside."

"This way." Emma led them back into the house. "The bedrooms are at the north end. The owner's suite is large and has an attached bathroom." Ed gave a superficial look around the room and then glanced in the bathroom.

Emma steered him into the second bedroom. "This is a nice sized room as well. It would hold another double bed. And it shares a Jack-and-Jill bathroom with a third, smaller room. What do you think, Ed?" She turned. Ed was staring out the window. She sighed. "Why don't we go across the hall? That room would make an ideal office." Ed pulled his gaze from the window and followed her.

Ed's mouth curved up slightly. "I could work from home in here."

Emma smothered a laugh. "What do you think?"

"It has definite possibilities. I would like to see the other house we have scheduled, but I may well put an offer in on this one. The commute to my office just off island wouldn't be bad from here. And I like that it's on high ground in case of storm surge. I don't think this house would flood."

"Those are all excellent observations." Emma was well into sales mode now. "We can talk more about this house after you see the last house of the day."

They drove a short distance to mid-island to their next appointment. Emma pulled into the driveway of a more modern ranch house. It had a large lawn but was land-locked.

Donovan looked around. "Ed's not going to like this one."

Emma's eyes twinkled. "I know. But sometimes you just need to show the client a property that doesn't work so that they realize they've found the one they want."

"Got it."

"Don't worry, this won't take long. Ed likes that last house. It has everything he wants. If I show him this one, it should clinch the deal."

Emma waved at Ed who had just pulled into the driveway. He got out and hurried over. "Sorry. I got separated in traffic."

"It's not a problem. We just got here ourselves." Emma unlocked the door and led them inside. Ed went straight to the back door and peered out. His face fell. There was no dock.

Emma shot an "I told you so" glance over Donovan. "Let's meet back at the office if you want to put an offer in."

"Yes, that's a good idea."

Emma and Donovan drove to the Rutledge building on Main Street with Ed following close behind them.

Emma powered up her computer and prepared the contract and offer on the house. After a few minutes she leaned back in her chair. "There, that's done. Ed, let me review the legalese with you." Ed pulled his chair closer to Emma so he could see the screen over her shoulder.

Donovan glanced at them. "Take your time. I've got some e-mails to catch up on."

Emma waited while Ed read through the document. "There, that's the whole thing. Any questions?"

"No. It's clear, thanks."

"Good. Just click here to electronically sign." She pointed to the screen. After Ed signed, she saved the form. "I'll e-mail this to the selling agent and call you as soon as I have news."

"Thanks, Emma."

Chapter 27

Donovan put his arm over his eyes to block the light shining through the blinds. It was a lot better than waking up at the crack of dawn to his military alarm. It took him a minute to remember where he was. In Emma's bed. Satisfaction pulsed threw him. Progress. Her arm draped over his stomach. He kissed her awake. "Good morning, beautiful."

"Umm, good morning. A girl could get used to waking up like this." Donovan kissed her shoulder. He continued farther south.

"Good. I'd like you to get used to this." He paused. "To us." Pleasure hummed through his body.

"Me too." She hitched a breath as his tongue circled her nipple.

"Hey, listen, I have to do something today. Matt is going to come over. I want you both to stay in the house. Don't open the door to anyone. And stay away from the windows. Would you do that for me?"

"Can't I go with you?" She stifled a moan as he kissed her low on her stomach.

"No, I'm afraid not. I want you here where I know you'll be safe."

"What are you doing? I don't want you putting yourself in danger for me." She writhed at his intimate touch.

"I love that you worry about me, sweetheart. But

you don't need to. I can take care of myself. But in any event, I'm just going to do some surveillance."

"If it's just a stakeout, why can't I go? Sounds harmless enough, right?"

"Just do this for me, Emma, please?"

"All right. It's been a while since Matt and I have just hung out. It will be good to spend some time with him."

"That's my girl."

He slapped her on the rear. "We had better get up and get dressed. Matt will be here soon." He got out of bed and reached a hand out to her. "Come on. Let's share the shower and save time and water."

Emma laughed. "Is that your best line?"

"No, but you're about to see my best moves." She couldn't stifle her giggle at his response. Grabbing a condom from the nightstand, he pulled her from the bed and scooped her up, carrying her into the bathroom. The oversized blue and white tile shower had multiple shower heads. As he walked into the shower area. Emma's giggles changed to shivers. He set her down and turned on the shower. Already fully erect, he ripped open the condom package and sheathed himself. He stepped under the water and pulled Emma in with him. He maneuvered her so she was under the rain shower and in the path of the lower shower heads.

She yelped. "Hey, the water's cold!"

"Hush. You'll forget all about the cold water. I promise." He took some liquid soap and ran his hands down her back, then turned to her front. He ran his hands over her breasts, paying particular attention to each nipple.

She moaned. "Don't stop. Please don't stop."

He gave a low chuckle. "You don't need to worry about that, kitten."

He continued farther down her body, hands circling her waist. Her head fell back, and water ran down her face. He reached her core and flicked her center. She shot off like a rocket. He adjusted her legs around his waist then thrust into her. At first, slowly, then gathering speed and power. The cool tiles of the shower wall rubbed her back. The pressure on her front built as the tempo of his thrusts increased. She exploded, and he followed her over the edge a moment later with a loud groan. He kept her legs around him as he waited for his breath to slow.

"Well?"

"Well, what?" Her eyes were vacant and unfocused.

"Were those some of my best moves?"

She laughed. "Fishing for a compliment? A little insecure?"

"Just making sure the lady is satisfied."

"Consider me well-satisfied." He let her down, steadying her as her legs wobbled. She toweled off.

Donovan wrapped a bath sheet around his waist and rubbed his jaw. "I guess I better shave." She leaned up to kiss his jaw.

"Don't shave on my account."

He pulled her into his arms. "Hmm... More of that, please."

Laughing, she pulled away. "We need to get dressed. Matt will be here soon."

Donovan glanced at his watch. "Hell. Any minute now."

"That's that, then." Emma went into the bedroom

167

and pulled out a thong from the dresser. She dropped the towel and wiggled into it. Donovan watched her, getting hard all over again. She shook her head at him and fastened her bra. He slammed the bathroom door.

"I'm dressed. It's safe to come out," Emma shouted at the closed door. He opened it and peeked out warily.

Emma wore a pale pink sleeveless sundress. It reached her mid-calf.

"Hey, coward. I'm headed downstairs." She opened the bedroom door and closed it soundly behind her.

A few minutes later Donovan came downstairs.

I made you a hot drink and sandwiches for your reconnaissance. See? I've seen the movies. I know how it goes."

He laughed. "I guess you do." The roar of a powerful engine announced an arrival.

"That must be Matt. Ann-Marie texted. She's going to come over too."

He walked to the front door and looked out the side window. "Yup, that's Matt. He's got a new car, I see. You couldn't miss hearing that one."

"You should talk. Boys and their toys."

He opened the door as Matt came up the sidewalk.

"Hey, man, nice ride. Thanks for coming. I appreciate you doing this." They bumped fists.

"Anything for you and Emma. How long do you think you'll be?"

He lifted one shoulder in a half shrug and frowned. "It's hard to say since I don't know what I'm looking for. It could be hours of watching nothing for a minute of excitement. Plan on staying all day. I've already given Emma her orders, but stay away from windows, don't let anyone in, and aside from letting Zeus out, don't go outside."

Matt shook his head. "That's pretty hardcore."

A muscle in Donovan's jaw twitched. "It's Emma's life we're talking about."

Matt's face froze. "Enough said. Count on me."

"Good. And be careful. Ann-Marie is coming over too. I get the feeling she could be a distraction, which might be good for Emma, but bad for security."

Donovan slapped Matt on the back. He took the supplies that Emma handed him and kissed her. "I'll have my phone on vibrate if you need to reach me. Enjoy your day with Matt and Ann-Marie. Just one more thing." He rooted around in the credenza in the living room.

"What are you looking for?" Matt looked at him curiously.

"I'm sure Jack keeps a pair of binoculars in here somewhere."

"He does have a pair, but they're not in there. He keeps them out on the patio to watch for North Atlantic Right whales as they migrate between Canada and here. I'll get them for you." Matt went outside and came back a minute later, handing a leather case to Donovan.

"Thanks. Now they'll help me watch another type of animal."

He headed out the front door and waited until he heard the sound of the deadbolt being engaged.

Chapter 28

Donovan parked the small compact car down a tree-lined side street a block from the High Road Church. He shifted his legs, trying to get more comfortable. He had exchanged the Rutledge Properties truck he was using while his own truck was being fixed for Mike's wife's car. He muttered a curse. *This car better blend in because I'm going to be crippled by the end of the day. I don't know how Mike tolerates it. But at least it has tinted windows.* He took out the binoculars and settled in for a long day.

From his position on the side street, he had a view of the front entrance. The congregation had repurposed an abandoned warehouse in an industrial part of the island into a place of worship. The gray metal roof and lack of windows robbed it of any aesthetic appeal. A platform where trucks could back up to unload their pallets occupied one end of the building. Now there was no need for delivery trucks. A discreet sign hung near the door announcing the name of the church.

He scanned the area with the binoculars, and his intuition pinged. There was no such thing as a coincidence. He glanced at his watch. He had timed his surveillance to coincide with the start of the ten o'clock service that morning. He had just trained the binoculars back on the front entrance when the door opened, and a man came out to greet the church members as they arrived. He recognized the pastor from the bail hearing. Donovan exchanged the binoculars for the camera with a zoom lens that he had also brought with him, clicking the camera rapidly, snapping photographs of groups of neat but inexpensively dressed parishioners as they filed inside.

The stream reduced to a trickle, and he glanced at his watch. Ten o'clock. *These folks are timely.* He poured himself a cup of coffee from the thermos and leaned back in the seat and waited for the service to end. Voices rumbled in the distance, and his eyelids fluttered open. Eleven thirty. *Yup. Right on time.* Churchgoers poured out, milling outside talking. He snapped more photographs of the crowd. When the last person left, he put the camera down and stretched.

Around two p.m. his head dropped with drowsiness, and he jerked awake. He unwrapped a sandwich and bit into it. The front door of the church opened, and a couple of men came out. He put the sandwich down and leaned forward. Both wore faded jeans and T-shirts. One man wore a baseball cap backward. Donovan reached for his camera and snapped a photograph. The men separated and walked to different cars.

At three p.m. Ken pulled up in his bland sedan and parked in front of him. His phone vibrated and Donovan picked it up.

"I'm here to relieve you."

"Thanks for splitting this with me."

"No problem. I plan to stay for a few hours, then have Mike keep watch overnight to see what if anything shakes loose. I'm not sure where this is going, but it doesn't feel right in my old cop bones."

"Thanks. I got photographs of everyone coming to the service, and the only action after that was two men leaving. I've got photographs of them as well."

"Great. E-mail them to me. Check with Emma and Matt. They may be able to identify the church attendees."

"I agree. See you later."

Chapter 29

Emma handed the remote control to Matt. "Why don't you pick a film, and I'll make some popcorn? We can have a movie marathon like we did when we were kids."

"Great idea. Let me see if I can find a B feature. They're so bad they're good." Matt clicked through the available movies before selecting one. Then he fiddled with the surround sound while Emma finished up in the kitchen. They settled down on the sofa in the living room. Zeus jumped up onto the couch and curled up between them. *The Monster From Beneath the Ocean* boomed from Jack's large screen television. Emma fed Zeus a few of the peanut butter dog biscuits that Elsa had made for him.

Three hours later, Matt stretched his arms in the air. "Huh. I don't think I'm going to go surfing for a while."

She laughed. "Those special effects were something else. But not in a good way. Why don't you see if you can find an encore movie, and I'll text Donovan to see how he's doing?"

Matt raised an eyebrow. "Checking up on him, sis?"

"Don't be silly… Well, maybe just a little bit. But I would like to know why he is so suspicious of High Road Church."

"Well, whatever it is, I'm sure he has a good reason. Donovan has good instincts." Matt channel surfed while Emma texted Donovan. Her phone pinged a response, and she opened the message.

"Hey, Donovan said Ken is taking over for him. He'll be back shortly. He just has to stop by Mike's house to get the truck back."

"Great. I'm having a hard time finding a movie to top that last one."

Emma giggled. "It was pretty good, wasn't it?"

Matt's expression turned sober. "How are you really, Emma? Tell me the truth."

She stared into the distance "In some ways, I'm great. Donovan and I are hitting it off. It's so great that sometimes I forget someone is trying to kill me." Her voice broke. "At other times, I think this thing with Donovan is too good to be true. And I remember that someone is out to hurt me." She continued in a monotone. "So I guess I don't know how to answer that."

Matt pulled her in to a hug. "I'm sorry you're going through this. But I trust Donovan. He'll keep you safe. And I hope this thing with him works out. He's a great guy. And he's waited a long time to be with you. That's determination and commitment. He's not anything like that loser Stephen."

Emma rolled her eyes. "You made your dislike of Stephen patently obvious through the years." She pushed a stray curl off her face. "Am I the only one who didn't know Donovan was interested in me?"

Matt chuckled. "Yeah, probably."

She winced. *So embarrassing.*

The doorbell chimed.

"I'll get it." Matt jumped up before Emma could move. He peered out the window. "It's Ann-Marie, my favorite barracuda."

"Now play nice." Emma shook her finger at him. "I don't know what it is between you. I can't figure out if you really dislike her. You protest too much. But I don't want any petty arguments today. Do you understand?"

Matt adopted an affronted stance. "I was nice. I called her my favorite, didn't I?"

Emma's features tightened. "Very funny."

Matt opened the door, and Ann-Marie breezed in with a bottle of wine. She kissed Matt on the cheek and eyed him up and down. "Hmmm...Ready to make me a cougar, sugar?"

"Not in this lifetime, Ann-Marie. We're much better off as friends." He suppressed a shudder.

"Shame." Ann-Marie's face fell in mock disappointment. "Well, maybe another time." She turned to Emma. "Join me for a drink."

"Absolutely."

"Where's Donovan? He's usually hovering over you. That man has it bad for you."

Emma hesitated. "He had to go out to talk to someone about a job. He's keeping it very hush hush."

Matt raised an eyebrow but didn't contradict her. He set three wine glasses on the table and handed a corkscrew to Ann-Marie. Deftly opening the bottle, she poured and settled with easy familiarity in an armchair, idly swinging her leg over the arm. She looked at Emma. "Hmm...That's quite a blush you've got going on. That answers my question whether you would mind if I made a move on him. Oh well. Plenty of fish in the sea. I'll do my trawling somewhere else." Her grin faded slowly but she glanced wistfully at Matt for a moment before turning away and taking a sip. "How is the police investigation going?"

"They don't tell me anything." It didn't feel right to talk about it. That wasn't her story to tell.

"Huh. Don't know why we pay our taxes if the police won't share anything. Well, never you mind." Ann-Marie took another swallow of her Chardonnay and looked at Emma contemplatively. "Do you still want that haircut? I brought my shears. I can cut it all off. Give you a real cute pixie cut."

Emma reached up and twirled a lock of hair. "I need a little more time to think about it. I don't want to do anything hasty and then regret it. It would take months to grow out."

"Sure, honey. Whatever you say." Ann-Marie's bosom shook as she laughed. "Things must be going well with Donovan. Come on, share with little ole me."

Emma's eyes flicked away from Ann-Marie for a moment. "There's nothing to talk about." *It feels like a private matter.*

Ann-Marie shrugged and turned to Matt, arching a brow. "How is my favorite man-whore?"

"Ann-Marie..." Emma warned.

"I'm just fine, Ann-Marie. Don't you have to be somewhere? Somewhere else, I mean." A flicker of sadness passed over Ann-Marie's face.

Emma crossed her arms and slayed Matt with a look of disgust. "Knock it off. Both of you."

Ann-Marie laughed and gulped the rest of her wine. "As a matter of fact, little brother is right. I've got to drop by the salon and unpack yesterday's delivery. I want to get everything put away before the stylists get in tomorrow morning. Otherwise they lose productive time."

"For a southern belle, you are quite the taskmaster." Matt observed caustically.

She lifted one shoulder. "I've got bills to pay just like everyone else. Maybe more."

She picked up her oversized handbag and leaned down to give Emma a hug. "We'll talk later when little ears aren't listening." She tugged on one of Emma's curls. "And whenever you decide you're ready for a new style, I'll be waiting with my scissors."

"Thanks, Ann-Marie. I'll see you soon."

She waved. "Bye, darlings."

Emma's mouth turned up at the corners. *We're complete opposites. But maybe that's why our friendship works so well.*

Chapter 30

Donovan returned Mike's car and picked up the Rutledge Properties truck. The wipers swished back and forth in a futile attempt to flick water off the windscreen. Water splashed up the sides of the truck as the tires hit a deep puddle. Donovan's grip on the steering wheel eased as he pulled into the driveway. He used the garage door opener he had borrowed from Emma's SUV to open the garage and pulled in. *Glad this didn't start earlier. It would have made visibility bad, and the photographs would be blurred.* Flexing his shoulders, he tried to ease some muscle tension. He stretched out a leg cramp before entering the house and finding Emma and Matt in the living room.

Emma looked up as he came into the room. "Oh, thank goodness you're back. We've been watching the storm roll in off the Atlantic. Driving conditions must have been terrible."

He kissed Emma on the cheek and sat down next to her. "Hi, kitten, Matt."

Donovan put his computer on the table. "It's quite a gale. I'm glad I didn't have far to drive." He gestured to his laptop. "I've got some photographs of church attendees that I'd like you to look at."

"Sure. What am I looking for?"

Donovan grimaced. "I don't know. I've just got a weird feeling about the church and want to learn as much about it as I can. Knowledge is power. Let me just download them." He sat down and powered up his computer.

Matt sat on the arm of the sofa and leaned over Donovan's shoulder. "Why don't you screencast them to the television? It will be easier for both of us to see. I might recognize some people too."

"Good idea, Matt." Donovan fiddled with the technology for a minute, then connected his computer to the television.

"Here we go. These first pictures are church members arriving for the morning service. Let me know who, if anyone, you recognize." Donovan put up the first photograph.

Emma and Matt both shook their head. "Don't recognize anyone."

He clicked to the next. "That's City Commissioner Randy Greene." Matt pointed out an older man with a woman and several preteen children. Donovan noted the name and number of the associated picture.

"Yes, I recognize his wife. That's Becky Greene."

"What do you know about Randy Greene?"

"He's Rawlings' cousin. He's the reason Ken had to hire Rawlings," Matt said.

"Interesting." Donovan didn't like the connection. A bit too convenient. "All right, let's move on." He advanced to the next photograph.

Emma pointed to a dark-haired woman. "That's Cindy Trent. I went to school with her. I believe she's a hairdresser. I don't know who the man is. I can't see her being involved. She was an all-around nice girl, at least in high school. I can't imagine that she has dramatically changed."

"Maybe not. But we don't know who the man is." Donovan glanced at Matt, who shook his head. They moved through more of the pictures.

"That image is so blurred I can't make out the faces."

"I know. People were moving. It was hard to get good shots."

Matt leaned forward. "Something about that guy looks familiar. But he's partially blocked." He shook his head from side to side. "I'm sorry. I just can't make him out."

"Well, we've identified several people. We've got something to think about. Just one more for you to look at. I took this one several hours after the church service ended."

"That's Miller!" Emma bounced off the sofa.

"Yes, it is. Remember, the church is sponsoring him, so we would expect to see him there." Donovan lowered his brows. "Do you recognize the man with Miller?"

Emma and Matt both leaned forward. Emma squinted.

"I can't see his face. With the baseball cap on, and he's kind of in the shadows, it's hard to tell." She heaved a sigh of disappointment. "No, I can't identify him."

Donovan pulled her into his side to hug her. "Don't worry. It was a long shot."

"Matt, do you have any idea who he is?"

"No." Matt pinched the bridge of his nose. "It's almost like he was doing his best not to be identified."

"All right. Thanks." Donovan shut the lid on his laptop. "Maybe Ken or Mike will have better luck. I'll talk to them tomorrow. I'm going to e-mail these photographs to Ken. He may be able to identify some of the people."

Chapter 31

"So tell me about this architect that Jack thinks so highly of." Donovan glanced over at Emma. "You look warm." He reached over and turned up the air conditioner in the car.

"Juan Garcia? He moved here from Atlanta a few years ago. His designs are innovative. He also incorporates a lot of energy efficient ideas. You'll like him."

Donovan flipped the truck's sun visor down to block the sun beating down on them from a sky devoid of clouds. Wind surfers, sails billowing, raced through the water, parallel to the road. He slowed, pulled into the driveway, and parked next to a flashy white sports car. A man dressed in the island uniform of polo and chinos leaned casually against the side of the vehicle. A pair of sunglasses rested on top of his head. His pale pink shirt set off his dark hair and bronze complexion.

Emma waved to him enthusiastically. "Juan, I'm so glad you were able to meet us." She reached up and kissed him on the cheek.

He grasped both her hands. "Always a pleasure, Emma!"

Laughing, she gently disentangled herself and gestured to Donovan. "Juan, this is Donovan Evans. Donovan is in the process of buying this house and would like to renovate and update it. Any suggestions you could make about what might be possible would be helpful."

Juan held out his hand. "Juan Garcia."

"It's good to meet you. I appreciate you taking the time to meet with us. I'm hoping that the house has potential for a significant renovation. It hasn't been updated since it was built in the 1980s."

"Of course. I'm happy to help out." He spread his hands wide in a welcoming gesture. "Jack has given a tremendous boost to my business with his work and recommendations. I'm happy to help a Rutledge connection. And don't worry about the age of the house. I've been known to work miracles."

"Ooh, let's start with the owner's bedroom. This way." Emma hurried down the hall. As she entered the bedroom, she spread her arms wide. "This room has such possibilities. What about larger closets for a start?"

Juan eyed the room speculatively. He tapped on several walls.

"Do you want walk-in closets?"

"Yes."

Juan glanced at Donovan. "These aren't structural walls. You could pull them out and reduce the size of the room just a little to give you maximum closet space. It's a good-sized room and could easily lose some square footage."

"That's exactly what I was thinking!" Emma's face glowed. "Now let's look at the bathroom." She opened the door. "Well, what do you think?"

He aimed a laser measure in several directions then jotted some notes on his e-tablet. "Do you want to keep the bathtub?"

"No, I don't think so." She paused. "Unless of course you want one, Donovan?"

A slow smile tugged at his lips. "What Emma wants, I want."

Juan nodded crisply. "Well, that makes it easy enough. I like a client who knows his or her mind. I would suggest removing the bathtub and putting in a large walk-in shower. I would move the bathroom vanity over there to make the bathroom more spacious. Then in the bedroom, I would also recommend updating the sliding glass door to the patio. You could put a large picture window in while still having a door to the outside."

Donovan's phone beeped. He glanced at the text message. "Will you both excuse me? Emma can carry on. She knows what I want."

Emma linked arms with Juan. "Come into the living room. I can't wait to hear your ideas."

After Emma and Juan had left the room Donovan punched in Ken's number.

"Any news?"

"Yeah. Not good though. Miller's dead."

"What. The. Hell." Donovan's grip on his phone constricted. "How? What happened?"

"Yeah, that about says it all. He was found dead at a homeless camp. Probable overdose, according to the uniforms who responded to the call." Ken's tone was flat.

"Convenient. That cuts the connection to whoever runs the operation, especially if it is a meth lab. It certainly wasn't Miller running the show." Donovan slammed his palm against the wall.

"I agree. Miller was acting under orders, and I'm

treating his death as suspicious. But even so, it's a blow. We were hoping he would snitch on his boss. No hope of that now."

"Damn. Double damn." A muscle in Donovan's jaw twitched. "What's the next step?"

Ken paused. "To be honest, I'm not quite sure yet. We've run up against a wall. Did Emma identify anyone from the congregation?"

"Yes, I e-mailed you the list of names, including Miller. I've got a picture of him meeting with someone. I'm not sure it's going to lead us anywhere though."

"I won't know until I see the list. There's always hope. Over the years I've learned that I never know what's important until, well, until it's important."

Donovan snorted. "Thanks for that illuminating explanation."

"I'll have an officer interview some of the church members in the course of looking into Miller's death. But I'll be honest with you. We really need to catch a break in this case. You probably know that the first few days are critical. After that the trail grows cold, and the likelihood of an arrest leading to a conviction greatly diminishes. And I've got to head back to Quantico. I've got a few weeks left in my course."

"I appreciate the time you've spent on this, Ken. Please keep me posted on any further developments. By the way, is Rawlings in charge of the investigation into Miller's death?"

"I'm afraid he is. Officially, that is. So you can expect a visit. You'll likely be his number one suspect."

"Something to look forward to."

"Mike will be keeping me updated. But if Rawlings becomes too much of a problem, let me know."

Donovan hung up and stretched some of the tension out of his neck before heading in search of Emma and Juan. He found them on the deck making plans for a plunge pool and an outdoor kitchen. *The look on her face makes it all worthwhile.* He put his arm around her waist and kissed her cheek. "Have you reorganized the house to your liking, Emma?"

Her cheeks flushed a light pink, and she darted a quick glance at him. "I have. I hope you don't mind."

"I don't mind at all. Juan, when can you send me plans?"

"I can have some ideas to you in a few weeks. I'll just need to come back and take more detailed measurements. I'll arrange with Emma to get the key when I'm ready."

"Great. That works for me." They shook hands, and Juan was on his way. "What do you think of the renovation plans, kitten?"

"I really like it. It will be a wonderful home." Her stomach fluttered.

"Good. I'm delighted to hear that. Your opinion is very important to me." He pulled her into a gentle hug. Inhaling her scent, he enjoyed the peace for a moment before releasing her. He sat down on the step of the porch and pulled her gently down to sit beside him. "I have some bad news. That was Ken on the phone. He wanted to tell us that Miller is dead. Likely an overdose. The only question is whether it was accidental or intentional. He's treating the death as suspicious."

"Oh my gosh!" Her eyes widened. "Do they have any leads?"

"Unfortunately not. I suspect I'm their principal

suspect because of the assault on you."

"So Rawlings will be after you." Her voice trembled.

"Probably." He scrubbed a hand over his face. "He's not a deep thinker, and I'm an obvious choice."

"Where does that leave us?"

"At a dead end. Literally." He pulled her into his side and rubbed her back soothingly. "Hey, Ken and I are on this. Don't worry." He used one finger to tilt her chin up. "We'll get this figured out. Meanwhile, I'll continue to keep you safe."

"But what about you? What if Rawlings arrests you?" Emma's voice cracked.

"He won't. He can't possibly have any evidence." His stomach lurched. *At least I hope not. I was alone most of yesterday.* He thought about some of the clearly erroneous arrests he had seen in the past.

Donovan kissed her on the top of her head. "But if he does, I want you to stay at Jack's house with Matt until Jack can organize other protection for you."

She nodded. The hair lifted on the back of his neck. She gave in too easily.

"I mean it, Emma. Look at me."

She continued to stare over his shoulder. Anywhere but directly at him. Finally she sighed.

"Yes, I promise. I'm not stupid. I want to stay alive."

He watched her with narrowed eyes. "Come on. Let's get back to Jack's. I need to do some thinking."

Chapter 32

Matt stopped by the next morning. "Mmm. I'll have some of your java specialty. It smells great." The aroma of the brew, spiced with cardamom, ginger, and cinnamon, filled the kitchen. Emma poured him a cup of her signature drink while Donovan updated him on the investigation into Miller's death.

Matt cupped the mug in both hands. "Is Emma still in danger? Could this be over?"

Donovan shook his head. "I think the danger is very real. I can't believe Miller was working alone. He simply didn't have the ability to plan and organize the meth lab."

Matt swore. "Where does that leave us?"

"Not in a good place. Listen, I assume Rawlings will haul me in for questioning. He may even arrest me. If that happens, I'll need you to watch over Emma."

"I will. But hopefully he won't be that stupid."

Donovan's mouth twisted. "Don't count on it."

Donovan's phone rang, and he glanced at the caller ID. "Here we go. Let the games begin."

He pressed the answer button. "Acting Chief Rawlings, what can I do for you?" He suspected the "Acting" in the title irritated him. He made sure to use it as often as possible.

"I'd like you to come to the station to answer some questions." Rawlings bit out each word.

"About what?" *Might as well not make things easy for him.*

"Miller was killed yesterday. You had a motive to kill him."

Donovan snorted. "I can save you some time. I didn't. So you can move on to other suspects."

Rawlings' tone sharpened. "Well now, Mr. Evans, I would still like to have a talk with you. I'll expect you in thirty minutes, or I'll send a patrol car to bring you in."

"If you put it that way." But Donovan was talking to a dead connection.

Emma walked into the room. "I've got to go have a chat with Rawlings. Remember our discussion. Matt is going to stay with you today." He put his hands on her shoulders. "Don't. Go. Out." He spoke slowly, emphasizing each word.

"I've got an appointment." Emma chewed on her bottom lip. "Janelle scheduled a new client for me."

He turned to Matt. "Can you go with her?"

"Of course. I've cleared my calendar of everything that I can't do by e-mail or phone."

"Thanks, Matt. Good man." They bumped fists.

Donovan backed the Rutledge Properties truck out of the garage. He couldn't wait to get his own vehicle back from the shop. Hitting the phone button on the console, he dialed a now familiar number. Ken picked up on the first ring.

"Rawlings has called me in for questioning. I'm heading there now."

"He's letting you come in voluntarily?"

"Yes, but I may not be walking out. Matt is staying with Emma."

"Understood. If anything happens, I'll see what I can do."

"Thanks." He disconnected the call and pounded the steering wheel in frustration.

Chapter 33

Matt drove Emma to the Rutledge Properties office in downtown Victoria City. The location on Main Street meant they had lots of walk-in traffic from tourists looking for homes. Matt pulled into the parking lot at the back of the multi-story historic building.

She smoothed out a wrinkle in her blouse as she got out of the car. A white shirt tied at the waist covered a lacy camisole. Her wide-legged black pants and sandals were stylish yet just practical enough for traipsing through backyards. She looked at Matt. For their client meeting he had put on a short sleeve polo shirt and khaki pants. At least his clothes were ironed, and he wasn't wearing shorts.

They walked around to the front of the building. Janelle Reed, their long-time receptionist, sat at her desk.

"Janelle, I have an appointment with a new client, Mindy Fairweather, in fifteen minutes. Can you let me know when she arrives?"

"Of course, Emma. It's good to have you back at work." Janelle beamed at her. "And look at you. You're looking wonderful. If I had known you were going to be in the office today, I would have made my chocolate brownies. I know you love them."

Emma grinned. "You're right. I do love them. My hips not so much. It's definitely good to be back. Can you set up a conference call with everyone for three this afternoon? We should put some more safety protocols in place for agents who are going out by themselves to show property."

Janelle made a note. "I'll get it set up right now."

"Thanks, Janelle. Matt and I will be in my office."

They walked past the front desk into the open plan office space. Residential sales were located on the first floor. Jeffrey Carter, the day's duty agent, had a landline phone tucked under his chin. He gave them a thumbs up as they walked by. Matt opened the door to Emma's office and gestured for her to precede him. She halted at the door. Acid burned in her stomach.

Matt quirked an eyebrow. She took a deep breath before striding in and taking a seat behind her desk. Matt shut the door.

"How are you doing so far, sis?" He flopped into one of the client chairs in front of her glass desk.

She sat and picked up a stray pencil and put it in the desk caddy. "I'm okay. The real test will be when I go to a property alone. Since you're here today, I think I'll be fine."

"There's nothing wrong with easing into this slowly. Besides, Donovan needs time to sort out this mess."

She closed her eyes for a moment. "You're right. It's like a bad dream. I just want to wake up and have it all over. Or better still, it never happened."

Matt came around the desk and gave her a quick hug. "It will be. Soon. Just hang in there." He leaned a hip on the side of her desk. "What's your client want?"

"Mindy Fairweather? She's looking for a large house for entertaining. She's a recent divorcee who received a large property settlement. She wants to move here and enjoy the good life. I believe she told Janelle her ex-husband was a surgeon." Emma lifted her chin. "She sounds like a bit of a cougar. Better watch out."

Matt smirked. "Hmm… Could be a nice distraction from Evelyn."

Emma sighed with exasperation. "You and Evelyn really need to stop the boomerang relationship. Anyway, at least wait until I finalize a sale with Mindy before you move in on her. I don't want anything to jeopardize my professional relationship with her."

Matt laughed. "Understood."

The phone on Emma's desk rang, and she picked it up. "Yes, Janelle, please send her back, thanks."

A minute later, Janelle ushered a woman in her late forties into Emma's office. Mindy Fairweather's artfully highlighted brunette hair framed her remarkably unlined face. She wore a white sleeveless sheath dress covered in palm trees, with high wedge sandals. Her oversized handbag had a prominent designer label.

Emma stood up to greet her. "Ms. Fairweather, welcome to Rutledge Properties. I'm Emma Rutledge, and this is my brother Matt. I hope you don't mind if he joins us today? He'll be taking notes for a training manual that he's writing for our agents."

"Oh, please call me Mindy, darlin'. It's a pleasure to meet y'all." She dazzled them both with a beauty queen smile. She let her hand linger just a shade too long when she shook hands with Matt. "I'd be happy to have such an experienced young man help us today. I'm sure I'll benefit from his energy."

Matt's gaze darted briefly to her legs. "I'm happy to be of assistance in any way I can, Mindy."

Emma had to restrain herself from pulling a face. "Please have a seat, Mindy. Would you like a coffee?"

"Maybe in a little while. Thank you, hon." Mindy sat down, crossing her legs gracefully and adjusting her dress hem as if attending a debutante ball.

"In your e-mail you said you were searching for a property that was suitable for large gatherings."

"Yes, I do love a good party, don't you?"

"Of course. And Victoria Island has a very active social life. I'm confident that you will love living here. You also said you wanted ample parking for guests and privacy from neighbors."

"That's right. I find it tiresome if neighbors complain about lots of cars when I have one of my little soirees."

"Within your price point, I've identified a couple different properties." Emma swiveled her computer to face Mindy. "Let's see if any of these interest you."

Emma clicked to open the details on the first listing. "Now this one is a penthouse right on the beach. It offers some of the amenities you requested including a swimming pool. It has direct beach access, and the views from the top floor are spectacular. It offers each resident two dedicated parking spaces, with spaces for guests on a first come first served basis in an overflow lot." Emma flicked through the interior photographs slowly.

Mindy tapped a French-manicured finger against her chin. "Well, it is a darlin' property, but in my experience condominium associations can be the very devil. I just don't think that would offer me the privacy I want."

"That's fine. Let me show you the next property."

Emma clicked and opened the next possibility. "This house is a generous size. It's almost four thousand square feet. The interior is fitted out to a very high standard. It has a swimming pool and hot tub. And the horseshoe driveway would give you plenty of parking for guests."

Mindy giggled. "Oh honey, how small do you think my get-togethers are? But it is a darlin' house. It might just do.

"Great." Emma jotted down the address on her notepad. "I'll contact the agent to schedule a viewing." She opened up the details of the final house. "This one is outside the city limits. It's an older two-story property. But it's on a large lot with lots of parking.

"It has a swimming pool as you requested. And an extra benefit. It has a small dock, so you have access to the intracoastal waterway." Emma moved to the next picture. "As you can see, the interior needs some remodeling. But this gives you the opportunity to make it your own."

Mindy tilted her head as she contemplated the house's potential. "I can see it has good bones. Before I married my ex-husband, I was an interior designer." She laughed softly. "That's how I met him in fact. I decorated his home." She waved her hand expansively. "This one has prospects. I'd definitely like to see it as well. The price seems right to allow for significant renovation."

"Wonderful." Emma relaxed back in her chair. A sense of euphoria rushed through her. She always got a buzz when she found the right property for her clients. "Let me organize these viewings. Would you like a coffee now? It will take me a few minutes to get these set up for you."

"That would be lovely, darlin'. Cream, no sugar."

Emma sent Janelle an instant message from her computer requesting the refreshments.

"Would you like to see some of the photographs of the island that we have?" Matt asked Mindy.

"Why yes." Mindy smoothed her dress over her hips.

"They're in the conference room next door." He stood and offered a hand to Mindy, who smiled like a cat that got the cream.

Emma signed into the realtor booking system to request showings for later in the day. Janelle knocked on the door and brought her coffee in.

"I've already taken Matt's and the client's drinks into the conference room." She mimed a cat clawing someone. "That man is such a player, but that Mindy is something else. She may eat him alive."

Emma stifled a laugh. "Thanks for the caffeine. I'm definitely going to need to be on my toes with this client. Matt volunteered to show her the 'etchings' in the conference room."

Janelle threw her hands up. "Does that line really work?"

"Apparently for Matt it does. I wouldn't have believed it if I hadn't seen it for myself."

A bell tinged on her computer. Emma pumped a fist in the air. "Success! Both viewings have been accepted. I've got her favorite one first too." Happiness flooded through her veins like a drug. Maybe the tide was turning in her favor.

Chapter 34

Donovan sat across from Chief Rawlings and one of his officers in a small interrogation room. The aged air conditioning system struggled to cool the room, and the body odor of the previous occupant hung in the air. The closed door did not completely shut out the clangor of phones from the bullpen. Donovan forced himself to relax his jaw. "How can I help you, Chief?"

Rawlings opened a file folder and flipped through his notes for several minutes. *He's just wasting time to try to make me nervous. Probably his grocery list. Amateur.*

He snapped the file folder shut. "I'd just like to go over a little background with you. You just left the military?"

"Yes. You know I did."

"Why did you come back?"

He pinched the bridge of his nose. *Stupid question.* Rawlings wanted to agitate him. No sense playing into his hands. He sat up straighter in his chair. "I grew up here. This is my hometown."

"What are you going to do here?"

Donovan crossed his arms across his chest. "Is any of this relevant to Miller's death?"

"Just answer the question." Rawlings bit out.

Donovan succumbed to temptation and rolled his eyes. "I'm exploring various employment opportunities."

Chief Rawlings slammed his palm down on the table. "You and Emma Rutledge have a thing going, don't you?"

"If by 'thing' you mean we're in a romantic relationship, then the answer is yes. Again, you know this. And it's not material."

"You were angry that Miller attacked Emma, weren't you? Any guy would be furious. A real man would do anything to ensure his woman was safe."

"Rawlings, that's straight from the interrogation playbook. You need to do better. But to answer your question, I'm an attorney. I don't believe in vigilantism. The justice system is the appropriate way to proceed."

Rawlings pointed his finger at Donovan. "But the law failed Emma, didn't it? The judge let Miller out of jail."

"Same answer, chief." Donovan tilted his head back and looked up at the camera in the ceiling.

"You had motive to kill Robert Miller."

"I've answered that already, Chief. I did not. I've said it before, and I'll say it again. I don't take the law into my own hands. I have faith in due process and the legal system."

"Where were you Sunday between the hours of nine p.m. and midnight?"

"I was with Emma at Jack Rutledge's home."

"Anyone else who can verify that?"

"Emma obviously can. Also, Jack has extensive surveillance cameras on the exterior of his property. Those will show that no one came or left on foot or by car."

"Video can be falsified."

Donovan waved his hand dismissively. "Check with his security company. They receive a direct feed in real time."

"You better believe we will. Hang tight." Rawlings picked up his file, and he and his officer left the interrogation room. The door slammed shut behind them.

Donovan glanced at his watch, then up at the camera hung from the ceiling. *Twenty more minutes. Then I'll force the issue. Rawlings doesn't have enough to charge me.*

Chapter 35

Emma drove Matt and Mindy to the first of the properties Mindy had requested to see. Emma turned into the long driveway of the waterfront home and parked in front of the "Old Florida" style house. She turned to Mindy, who sat in the passenger seat.

"What's your first impression of the house?"

Mindy tapped her finger on her leg. "Why, it's just darlin'. So charming. And such a long driveway with lots of parking. I just can't wait to see the possibilities inside."

"Excellent. Let's take a look."

They all got out of the SUV and headed to the house. Emma opened the lockbox and got the key out. She unlocked the front door and ushered Mindy in. Matt trailed behind.

"That chandelier! That is so precious." An elegant crystal chandelier hung over the entry area. Five tiers of crystal glass prisms glimmered and sparkled.

"Well, the good news is that the light is considered a fixture and would come with the house."

Mindy wandered into the next room. "This would make an elegant formal parlor." She looked at the floor and frowned. "Of course, I'd need put in some hardwood. I just can't wait to see the rest of the house."

"Of course. The kitchen is this way. It's quite large. As you know, you could give it a real facelift if you install granite countertops. That would add real value to the property."

"Yes, I can see that." Mindy opened the door to the pantry and peered in. "Lots of space." She closed the door.

"Where's the main bedroom?" Mindy gave Matt a side glance. "I do like a well-appointed owner's suite. Don't you?" Emma raised an eyebrow at Matt.

"It's upstairs. Let's go take a look." They returned to the foyer and the elegant double staircase.

"This stairway adds a certain sophistication to the property." Emma pointed out the features as she led the way to the master bedroom. She gestured to the picture window. "You can see all the river traffic from here." She stared at the closed bedroom door. The jackhammering of her heart reverberated loudly in her ears. A sheen of sweat shone on her forehead. She reached out for the door knob with a trembling hand. Glancing over her shoulder, she locked eyes with Matt. She hadn't fooled him.

Matt turned so his body partially obscured Emma and spread his arms wide. "Can you picture yourself walking down this staircase to join your party guests? That would be quite an entrance."

Mindy winked at him. "Honey, I like the way you think."

Emma flashed a half-smile at Matt. She opened the door slowly. Goosebumps erupted on her arms. *It's different this time. I'm not alone. There is nothing to be afraid of.* She paused in the entry to the bedroom. Impatiently, Mindy brushed past her and clapped her hands. "This is perfect. I can just see my furniture in here. I have a darlin' chaise lounge that might fit in that corner." She pointed to the back. She paused. "But is it big enough?" Mindy opened her capacious handbag and started fishing around for something. Her brows drew together.

"Matt, honey, would you mind? My tape measure must have fallen out of my bag in the car. Would you be a darlin' and go look for it?"

"I've got one." Emma pulled a measuring tape out of her purse. "I always carry one. Lots of clients want to check room sizes."

Mindy's smile slipped. "Bless your heart, honey, but I have a laser measure that will give me exact measurements. I never work without it."

Matt raised his hands. "No problem. I'll just go check the car. I won't be a minute." Emma handed him her keys. He trotted out of the bedroom and down the stairs.

Something thudded loudly followed by a cry of pain.

"Matt! Matt! Are you okay?" She ran to the door to follow Matt downstairs.

A thump sounded behind her. "Stop, bitch."

Emma ground to a halt and whirled around. Mindy's handbag was on the floor. Emma pulled her focus away from the purse and up to Mindy. Mindy's finger was wrapped around the trigger of a gun, pointed directly at her. Her heart drummed in her chest.

"W-what's going on?" She jerked her hand to her throat. Her voice came out in a croak. "What are you doing?"

Mindy's face twisted. "You've been a complete pest. And a stupid one as well if you have to ask. It's time to end this. Now throw me your cell phone."

*Why did I think she was attractive and stylish? Attitude is everything I guess.* Emma fought down a hysterical laugh. She squeezed her eyes shut. *Maybe this is a hallucination.* She opened them, and Mindy was still pointing a gun at her. *Nope.* She reached into her purse and pulled out her mobile. She tossed it in Mindy's direction.

Mindy sneered. "We had to get rid of a perfectly good employee thanks to you. You've got to pay for the trouble you've caused us." Her hand with the gun shook.

Emma flinched as the gun wavered. Sweat beaded on her forehead and dripped down her face despite the air conditioning. "Please let me go see Matt. He could be hurt. Please, he has nothing to do with this." Bile rose in her throat, and she swallowed with difficulty.

"Oh, he's hurt all right. And it's your fault. You shouldn't have brought him with you," Mindy taunted her, eyes like cold steel.

Emma blinked rapidly.

*Don't hyperventilate. Stay calm.* She counted four breaths in and out. *Think. Damn it. Think.*

"I knew that accent was overdone. Is your name even Mindy?" Sarcasm dripped from her words.

"No. Mindy is such a stupid name, isn't it? But you bought the whole act, didn't you? Greedy bitch. All you could see were dollar signs in selling me a house," Mindy mocked her.

Emma stared at the gun as if it were a cobra. "Put the gun down. This doesn't have to end badly. Let us walk out of here. We won't go to the police. Just leave."

Mindy sniggered. "You're not in charge here,

Emma. Enough stalling. Move." She gestured with the gun, and Emma backed slowly to the bedroom door before turning to walk down the stairs. Her legs shook, and she clung to the stair railing to keep herself steady. When she reached the bottom, she turned the corner and cried out.

"Matt!" She ran over and knelt beside him. A crimson pool surrounded his head. "Matt, can you hear me?" She quickly removed the shirt covering her camisole and held it gently against his head to stem the flow of blood.

She turned to Mindy, her eyes brimming with tears. "Please! I've got to get him medical help."

Mindy's nostrils flared. "Fool. Get up. It's time to go."

"You can't leave Matt here. He's hurt."

"Well, you're right on one count. I can't let him stay here."

A door from the backyard opened, and a stocky man with an unkempt beard that formed a hairy "V" over his chest came in. He wore sideburns and had pulled his hair into a ponytail. His faded jeans had holes in the knees, and his black T-shirt was emblazoned with skull and crossbones. "Where have you been?" Her voice was laced with annoyance.

"Your text message didn't give us a lot of time to make arrangements. Had to help Caleb tie up."

"No names, you idiot. I'll just call you Skully." Mindy hissed. She gestured toward Matt. "Grab his phone, then pick him up and throw him in the boat."

He leaned down and heaved Matt over his shoulder. His knees buckled as he stood up. "Umph..." Matt's head flopped.

"Hurry up. We need to be quick about this."

Skully staggered under the deadweight. "Fuck. He's heavy. I'm doing the best I can. You should have planned this better." He stumbled out the back of the house, his chest heaving.

"Fuck you and the horse you rode in on." Mindy gave him a hard smile.

She motioned with the gun for Emma to follow. "You too, missy. Get moving."

"I'm going. I'm going." Emma held her hands up. She followed slowly, stumbling on the uneven ground. Her eyes darted around. *No point in making a run for it. I can't leave Matt. We get out of this together or not at all.* Her chest tightened at the thought, and she struggled to breathe.

They reached the end of the backyard just as Skully lurched forward and lost his grip on Matt, who plummeted to the ground. A speedboat rocked side to side in the gusts of wind.

"You, get in first." Emma leaned down, put her hand on the side of the boat, and stepped aboard. She stumbled and dropped to her knees as the craft rocked under her weight. Skully grunted as he picked Matt up again. Blinking the sweat out of his eyes, he leaned over and dropped Matt over the side. Emma dove to protect Matt as he fell, and his weight pinned her to the floor. The vessel rocked violently, threatening to capsize.

"Moron," Mindy hissed.

"Give me a minute." He bent over with his hands on his thighs, panting.

A blond man with a crewcut snorted from the cockpit. The unlikely looking thug wore wraparound

205

sunglasses, a white T-shirt, and cargo shorts. "The boat will stabilize. But don't do that again."

Skully climbed into the aft, and Mindy followed. She untied the mooring and threw the rope onto the deck. Caleb hit the throttle, and they roared away from the dock leaving a wake in their path. The shorebirds in the marsh flapped their wings in protest. The jerk as it pulled away dislodged Matt, who moaned faintly. *He's too quiet. Oh my God. I can't lose him.*

Emma pressed her blouse against his wound again while her thoughts raced. *I need a plan. Donovan would know what to do.* A small sigh of relief escaped when Caleb steered away from the ocean. *At least they're not going to shoot us and dump us overboard.* She stifled a hysterical laugh. *At least not yet. They can't afford to let us live. We can identify them. I need a plan. But it's three against one. Matt won't be able to help.*

Her heart pounded so fiercely she thought her chest might explode. *I'm so sorry, Matt, that I got you involved in this. Will we ever see our family again? I wished I had gone after Donovan a long time ago. Now we won't have a chance.*

She didn't know how long they had been traveling before the vessel slowed. A line of houses with piers, much like the house where she had first been assaulted, bordered both sides of the river. *Damn. No familiar landmarks.* Caleb angled the watercraft toward one of the docks. He threw the rope to a tall, skinny man wearing a baseball cap backward and an unlit cigarette hanging out the side of his mouth. He expertly caught the rope and moored the vessel. He held a hand out to help Mindy alight.

Matt whimpered and reached up to touch his head.

His hand was sticky with blood. Caleb looked at Mindy. "He's coming around."

"Well, good. He should be able to walk then, shouldn't he?"

Emma reached down and gave Matt a hand as he tottered and tried to stand. His pupils were dilated, and his features were slack. The boat rocked slightly, and he started to heave. "He's going to be sick."

"He better throw up in the water, or I'll shoot him myself."

Emma frantically hauled him toward the side but slipped, and he fell. She scrambled until she gained leverage on the slippery floor, then lugged him back to his feet. Worn out from the exertion, she tipped over pulling him with her to the edge. She held his head as he vomited into the river.

"You dodged that bullet." Mindy broke out in a deranged laugh.

*Oh my gosh. She's certifiably crazy. I've got to get us out of here.*

"Come on. Get out. Caleb, help her get her brother out of there." Caleb stepped forward, put his arm under Matt's shoulder. Skully grabbed him from the other side. Together they dragged him onto shore. Emma climbed out behind them. Caleb and Skully let Matt go, and she rushed to catch him, staggering under his weight.

"Matt, come on. Walk with me. You can do this," she whispered urgently to him. His head lolled, and his eyes stared blankly. He moved his legs slowly, and together they lurched side to side behind the kidnappers. Mindy followed with the gun.

"Put them in the boat house. We'll dump them in

the ocean after dark."

Emma bit back a scream as fear washed over her like an arctic wave. Caleb opened the door of what looked like a dilapidated shack near the dock and pushed them inside. Emma fell and dragged Matt down with her. Her captor slammed the door, and she heard the snick of the lock. She blinked while her eyes adjusted to the dimness, made visible by the streamers of light. She bent over Matt.

"What's going on?" Matt's eyes drifted shut.

Fear twisted her gut. *He just has to be okay.*

"Shh…Just rest a minute, Matt, while I see what I can figure out here." She put her shoulder against the door and pushed. It didn't budge.

Even if she could get them out, how would she get Matt away? The house was not an option. That's where the crazy woman and her thugs were. Could they swim out? She rejected that idea. She could swim, but she didn't think Matt could in his condition.

Leaving him behind while she went to get help was not an option. She felt with her hands around the walls of the shack. She bumped into a pull chain and yanked it. *Thank goodness.* The single lightbulb gave enough light for her to make out the interior of the shed. *Damn.* The construction was not quite as ramshackle as she had thought. *Please God don't let them see the light.* A canoe leaned against the back wall. Could she get the door open and the canoe out and launched, all before the people in the house heard them? They would surely hear her dragging it out of the building.

A tinge of hysteria bubbled up. It was an impossible task. *Come on, come on. Think, damn it. What other options are there? What about a weapon?*

A rusted toolbox sat on top of a pile of debris in the corner. She tugged the lid up. A hammer. Screwdriver. Wrench. They might come in handy.

Matt roused and turned his head, moaning. "Matt, stay with me." She put the wrench in his hand. He grasped it, but his hand fell limply to the ground. "Use this to hit them over the head if they come near you." It was not great. But it was a plan.

A ramp led down to the water on one side of the building. At the end of the incline was a door somewhat like a metal garage door, extending down into the water. Would it be possible to swim underneath the door and come up on the other side? She could then unlock the main door and get Matt out. *I'm a fairly strong swimmer. If I can pull him in a rescue position and swim with him a few houses down, we might be able to get help.* She looked around again. A life preserver hung on the wall. She could use that to keep Matt afloat while she swam with him. If she stayed close to shore, she might avoid the pull of the current. She turned to Matt who was watching her.

She knelt in front of him. "How are you feeling?"

"Head hurts." His face contorted with pain.

"I know. I'm sorry." Tears brimmed up and ran down her face. "Listen, we have to get out of here."

"I'll second that." Matt touched his head and winced.

"I'm going to try to swim under the garage door and come up on the water side. I'll then smash the lock with this hammer and open up the door on the land side." She handed him the life preserver. "Hang on to this. I'll float you down the intracoastal."

"That's crazy, Emma. The current will be too

strong." Matt protested weakly even as his voice shook.

She wiped her face and sniffed. "Matt, look at me." His eyes drifted shut. He slammed his hand to the floor to steady himself and turned toward the sound of her voice. "It's our only option," she said urgently. "I'm a good swimmer. We don't have to go that far to get help. If we hug the riverbank, hopefully we can avoid the worst of the current. We've got to get out of here. They plan to kill us."

"Yeah, but what about alligators?"

"The intracoastal is brackish. They don't like salty water."

His head fell forward. She leaned in. "Matt, what did you say?

He gave a shaky laugh. "That's the conventional wisdom. But they forgot to tell the alligators that."

Emma hugged him, careful to support his head. "We'll be careful. We're due for some good luck."

"Be careful, sis." She nodded, a lump in her throat. With one last look she went down the ramp, took a deep breath, and slipped into the water.

She dove deep. The door extended down farther then she had hoped. She kicked down again in the murky water. Pressure built in her eardrums, and a weight pressed her chest. She reached out as she went, feeling the metal door as she descended.

Finally, she could feel the bottom of the door. She went underneath and thrust frantically toward the light. Her lungs strained until she thought they would burst. She scissored her legs feverishly and exploded out of the water. Gasping for air, she treaded water. When she regained her breath, she kicked toward the dock, then pulled herself up and peeked over the edge. She looked left then right. When she didn't see anyone, she swung up and flopped onto the dock. She collapsed, panting. After catching her breath, she crawled toward the locked door.

Emma scanned the area for people, and her gaze darted past the speedboat. *Damn.* She tamped down a manic laugh. *They had left the key in the ignition.* She looked around again. She didn't see anyone, so she slithered around the side to the door. The lock mechanism looked solid. She wasn't sure smashing it with the hammer would work, and the noise might attract attention. *Damn. I've come so far.*

Her heart thundered in her chest. They would keep the key handy. She looked around and down. Her hands shook as she lifted the various stones near the door. She got lucky on the third rock. *Even criminals needed to keep a spare key handy.* She smothered a laugh at the absurdity. She stole a quick glance toward the house. Had she made any noise? Still clear. She inserted the key in the lock and turned it. Click. Her knees buckled, and she reached out to steady herself against the wall before opening the door.

"Matt."

"Thank God, Emma."

"Here. Put your arm around my shoulders. Change of plan. We're leaving in style."

She swayed as she took the brunt of his weight. They shuffled out the door, the wooden deck creaking under their feet. *Please God, don't let them hear us. Don't let them look out the back windows of the house.* She bent Matt over backward, and he tumbled into the boat. He bit out a moan. "I'm sorry that hurt, Matt. Hang on."

Emma stepped up and over the side but lost her footing, landing hard on her shoulder on the damp floor. She hissed at the pain. Drawing a shuddering breath, she grabbed the side to steady herself. She pulled herself up, wincing as if a red-hot poker shot down her arm. Then she untied the line and threw the rope clear so it didn't tangle with the propeller. She turned the key in the ignition, and the engine coughed and spluttered. *Damn.* Her pulse ratcheted up from racing to rocket speed.

She glanced at the house. The back door opened, and Caleb ran out. Panic clawed at her insides, and she froze. *He was coming for them. He was going to kill them. They would be shark bait. Get a grip.* Pop! *Oh my God. They're shooting at us.* She dived to the floor and reached up to turn the key. This time the engine roared to life. She clung to the side of the boat and crouched over. *Thank God for those fishing trips with Dad.* Pop! Pop! She ducked instinctively at the sound of the gunshots.

"Stay down!" she screamed over the noise of the motor. She turned her head to see if Matt heard her, but he lay face down on the floor, and she couldn't tell if he was conscious. *He has to be okay. He just has to be.* She pushed all thoughts to the back of her mind. *Concentrate. You're not out of this yet.* She pushed to maximum throttle, and the engine thundered into life. She steered blindly away from the dock.

## Chapter 36

Donovan glanced at his watch. *Damn it. Rawlings is just burning time.* He texted Emma. No response. He scrubbed a hand over his face. Something was off. He tried Matt. He didn't answer either. His gut churning, he dialed the Rutledge offices, but it went straight to voicemail. He pulled up Ken in his contacts and hit call.

"I can't get in touch with Emma or Matt. I'm worried. They were going out with a client to look at properties, but that was hours ago. Rawlings is just wasting my time. I'm leaving here. I don't have a good feeling about this. I'm headed to the properties she was showing."

"Text Mike the address, and I'll call him and tell him to get there ASAP. He can meet you there."

"Thanks. I'll let you know what we find out."

The door opened, and Rawlings and his officer came back in.

"Time to finish our little chat."

"I'm leaving, Rawlings. You don't have enough to charge me. You're just fishing, and frankly, not doing it well."

Rawlings opened his mouth and then closed it again. He looked at his officer, who shook his head. Turning back to Donovan, he slammed his file folder shut. "Don't leave town, Evans." Donovan didn't say anything. Rawlings was the type who needed to have the last word.

Donovan shouldered past Rawlings and hurried back through the bullpen to the reception area. He rushed toward the exit, gaining speed as he went, and by the time he reached the door, he was running. Sweat soaked his shirt, and acid burned in his stomach. *The whole interview with Rawlings just stank. Almost as if Rawlings was stalling or trying to keep him occupied. Emma.* He ran out the police station and jumped into his truck. He dialed the Rutledge Properties office again.

"Rutledge Properties. We find the house of your dreams. Janelle speaking."

"Janelle, this is Donovan. Where's Emma?"

"Donovan, it's good to have you home."

"Janelle, listen, I'm afraid Emma's in trouble. Where is she?"

"She and Matt took a client to see a few houses." Janelle glanced at her watch. Closing time. "Come to think of it, I would have thought they would be back by now. They left right after lunch. And she didn't appear for a conference call that she scheduled. I had to cancel it. I just assumed she got busy with her client."

"Text me the addresses that she was going to. And if they come back, or she calls, please contact me immediately."

"Of course. Is everything all right?"

Donovan didn't have time to reassure her. "Got to go. Thanks." He hung up. He glanced down at the first address and typed it into his GPS. His phone rang.

"Yeah?"

"It's Mike. Ken filled me in."

"Meet me at this address. He rattled off the street

and house number. Putting the truck in gear, he peeled out of the police station. *Focus.* It wouldn't help Emma if he were in an accident.

"I'm ten minutes out. Maybe less."

"Okay, I'll meet you there." Donovan expertly weaved through the early evening traffic, dodging a car whose driver dithered at every intersection. He banged the steering wheel with the palm of his hand as a driver pulled out in front of him, then failed to get up to speed.

"Come on, come on." He whipped the truck around the slow-moving car, stomped on the gas pedal, and swerved around a golf cart driving in the bike lane until he reached the turning for Atlantic Boulevard. The tires on his truck squealed and it fishtailed in an oil slick as he rounded the corner. He straightened the truck and looked for his turning on the left. Turning onto Pelican Drive, he scanned the house numbers. "There!" He jumped on the brakes and turned into the driveway.

He dialed Mike and said, "I'm pulling up now. Emma's car is in the driveway. I'm going in." He parked his truck next to Emma's SUV. Jamming the phone in the pocket of his cargo pants, he grabbed his gun out of the glove compartment. Donovan opened the truck door and slipped out, leaving the door ajar. Bending over, he ran to the house and peered through the window adjacent to the door, then tried the door. Unlocked. He pushed the door open and dove through. Silence. He cleared the house room by room. Empty. He looked out the upstairs window. Mike pulled into the driveway and parked next to Donovan's truck. Donovan hurried down and opened the door.

"No one's here. But we've got blood." Donovan pointed at the floor. "Damn it." Donovan clenched his fists. "Where are they?"

"We can check with the neighbors. See if they saw any other cars," Mike suggested. "I'll need to call this in."

"I hate to get that bastard Rawlings involved. But I agree." Donovan pointed at the blood trail on the ground. "There are drops leading to the back door." They walked along the edge of the room, trying to avoid contaminating the scene. "They left on the river."

"How does that help us?" Mike muttered a curse.

"Well, they seem to have a pattern of using unoccupied homes that are for sale. I'll call Jack and get him to pull up all the vacant homes that have water access. Do the police have a boat?"

"Yes. I'll get Ken to authorize its use. Maybe we'll get lucky. Come on. It's kept at the city-owned launch at the north end of the island." Mike pulled up a number on his cell and stepped away from Donovan to speak on the phone. After a minute, he hung up.

"It's all set. Let's go. Follow me."

Donovan raced to his truck. He started the engine and threw the vehicle into reverse. He pulled out quickly and followed Mike. Steering the truck into a hard right, the tires squealed as he turned into the road leading to the public launch area. He pulled up next to Mike's truck, jumped out, and ran to Mike. Mike glance over his shoulder. "Took you long enough."

"Not funny."

Mike punched a code into a keypad to access the storage facility. "Okay, here we go. Back your truck up to the sliding door. We'll hitch the boat and tow it to the launch ramp."

"Got it." He pulled his dually forward and then

backed it up toward the sliding door of the building.

Using hand signals Mike indicated he should back up farther. Watching carefully, he continued to reverse until Mike waved him to stop. He tapped his fingers on the steering wheel. "Hurry up, man." Finally, Mike signaled the all-clear. He towed the boat to the launch area and reversed down the slope. Mike jumped in and unhooked it from the tow.

He stomped on the gas, and the truck jerked away from the water. He abandoned it next to the ramp. Mike gave him a hand and pulled him on board.

"Any ideas which way they might have gone?"

Donovan's phone pinged. He glanced at the text message.

"It's from Jack. He suggests we head south down the intracoastal." The house that was for sale was closer to the mouth of the waterway. There will be more houses south. Extra opportunities for them to moor. *Maybe. Unless they went out to the ocean.* It was unthinkable. "Can you put out a call to the Coast Guard? In case they went out to the ocean? In case we're wrong?"

Mike gritted his teeth and picked up his phone to make the call. Steering with one hand, he held the phone to his ear with the other. He shouted into the phone over the noise of the engine.

Donovan scanned the area. Marsh grass lined both sides of the waterway. Houses built back from the riverside had long docks that reached out through the marsh to the water. Some had watercraft of all varieties docked. Others were uninhabited.

Donovan looked around at the surprisingly deserted channel. Finishing his call with the Coast

Guard, Mike hung up and put it in his pocket. He turned to Donovan.

"They're sending a helicopter out to run search patterns. But it's a problem. We don't know when they left," he yelled over the noise of the motor. "They could have traveled quite a distance."

Donovan grimaced. "Tell me something I don't know."

"Sorry, man."

"Let's hope they came this way. Keep on the lookout for anything unusual. There aren't many boaters out today. Less to check, but also no witnesses."

He pulled his binoculars out of one of the pockets of his cargo pants. His knuckles were white as he scanned both sides of the waterway. He flexed his fingers. He had to find her. Fate couldn't be so cruel to them both. *She had to be okay.* He panned the binoculars over the river, past white egrets and vivid pink Rosetta spoonbills fishing for their dinner. *How can it look so peaceful while my world is falling apart?* He gestured for Mike to slow down as he spotted a vessel that had been run ashore and grounded. "Look! There!"

Mike pointed with one arm, his other on the wheel. "I see it." He slowed and steered toward the riverbank. He throttled down farther and maneuvered to pull up alongside the dock. *Why didn't they tie up?* Jumping out, Donovan caught the rope Mike threw to him. Mike killed the engine and leaped out. Donovan ran over to the stranded speedboat and peered in. "Blood." He sniffed. "Oil. I don't think it's been here that long. Let's go up to the house."

"Hostiles?"

"Likely. Let's approach from the side. We can use the marsh grass for cover. Just don't piss off any alligators."

"Funny, Donovan. It's the water moccasins I'd worry about. I'll take the west side."

Donovan headed east. He bent over in a crouch and made his way through the tall grass. The stench of sulfur from the decaying vegetation assaulted him. Sweat dripped off his face. He exhaled deeply as he reached the end of the wetland, then crossed the ground from the marsh grass to the house in a run. Mike bent over and approached the house from the opposite side.

Donovan peered in a side window. His heart hammered in his chest. Emma stood in the kitchen with an elderly woman. The other woman's white hair formed a cap around her face. She wore an old-fashioned housecoat and slippers. Bending over Matt, she held a towel against his head. A siren blared in the distance.

The door creaked and Emma jerked. "Donovan!" She screamed, ran to him, and threw her arms around him. "You found us! I knew you would."

"Did they hurt you?" Donovan ran his hands down her body, searching for injuries.

"I'm fine. But Matt has a head injury. Mrs. Wilder has called an ambulance."

Mike came in the back door.

Donovan locked eyes with the elderly woman. She dipped the washcloth into a bowl of water. "Indebted, ma'am."

"Oh posh. It's nothing." She waved her hand in a dismissive gesture. "This is the most excitement I've had in a long time. When Mr. Wilder gets home, he'll never believe my story. That this young lady was kidnapped, stole a boat, and ran out of gas. She was marooned just feet from our dock! Mr. Wilder is going to regret going to his fishing club meeting when he learns about this adventure."

The low rumble of voices came from the front, and a pounding on the door signaled an arrival.

"Good. It's the ambulance." Mrs. Wilder handed the washcloth to Emma and started to move toward the front door.

Emma's heart beat wildly in her chest. Panic clawed at her. "Wait, Mrs. Wilder! What if it's them? What if they found us? Check the window. Make sure it's the ambulance."

"We can hear the siren, kitten." Donovan pushed a curl off her face.

"I know." Emma's voice trembled. "But they're everywhere."

"All right. Hold up, Mrs. Wilder. We can't be too careful." Donovan passed Mrs. Wilder to reach the front door first. He looked out the peephole. "It's the ambulance." He opened the door and stood back. "Thank God you're here."

Two emergency services personnel rushed in the door. They wore the short-sleeve blue uniforms of the fire department. The lead medic had a tattoo sleeve on one arm and Semper Fi on the other arm. He adjusted his medical bag over his shoulder. His partner's ponytail swung as she pushed a stretcher. "Where's the patient?"

"In the kitchen. This way." Donovan waved them through.

"Hi, I'm Greg. I'm going to take a look at your

injury, okay?" The medic set his bag down, put on rubber gloves that partially covered his tattoos, bent over Matt, and parted his hair around his wound.

"What's your name, sir?"

"Matt Rutledge."

He looked him over, prodding gently, then took a pen flashlight and shined it in his eyes. "Follow the light." He nodded in satisfaction. "Head lacerations bleed a lot. He'll need to go for an MRI of course. But I think he'll be fine." He glanced at his partner. "Janie, can you get me the gauze roll?"

His partner leaned down to rummage in the kit bag. "You didn't restock, so that means you're on cleaning duty tonight. But you're in luck. There's one left." She threw him the bandage roll.

He caught it easily. "Thanks." He wrapped Matt's head. "How does that feel?"

Matt touched his head. "Bandage feels fine. Of course, my head hurts."

Janie laughed. "Good to see you've got a sense of humor about this."

"All right. Let's get him on the gurney." Janie lowered the stretcher. Matt held a hand up. "It's all right. I can do this." He shuffled onto the stretcher and lay back.

Janie locked the safety rails, and they transported him out to the ambulance.

"Can I ride with him?" Emma put her hand on Matt's arm.

The medic shook his head. "I'm sorry, ma'am. Insurance rules." He closed the door of the ambulance.

Donovan ran his finger down her cheek. "We'll get you there, Emma. Mike, we need to secure the evidence and get to the hospital."

"I'm already on it. I've called off all the searches, and I've got help on the way. My buddy should be here any minute. I'll get him to take you to the hospital. I've also got our forensic team coming out to process everything." Tires crunched on the gravel driveway, and Mike looked out the window. "It's the crime scene unit. Ma'am, I hope you don't mind if they examine the speedboat here before any evidence is lost due to possible rain."

"Of course not. I'll put some coffee on for them." She bustled around the kitchen.

"That's very kind, thank you. Coffee is always appreciated."

"You go right ahead and do what you need to do. I'll let you know when it's ready." She shooed him out the door.

Mike opened the door and directed the forensic team around the back. "I'll be out in a minute, guys."

"Sergeant, take Emma and Donovan to the hospital, and take Emma's statement. I'll meet you there when I'm done here."

The officer gestured for Emma and Donovan to follow him out to the patrol car.

Chapter 37

They found Matt in the emergency room in a cubicle separated from the hectic triage area by a curtain. Emma looked at the pixie haired nurse sitting at the nursing station.

"Can we go in?"

"The doctor is with him now. Let me check." She poked her head behind the curtain and then waved them in. An older woman in a lab coat that covered a simple blouse and black pants looked up from the chart she was reviewing. Her high-top sneakers clashed with her gray hair.

"You must be Emma. Everyone at the hospital is talking about you. I hear you had quite an adventure."

"I am, and we did. How is he, doctor?" Emma's brow furrowed.

The doctor adjusted the stethoscope around her neck. She touched Matt lightly on the shoulder. "I'd like to keep your brother overnight just to be careful. I want to keep an eye on him. I'll have the nurse organize his transfer to a bed."

Matt tugged at his hospital gown. "I don't need to stay overnight."

Emma shook her head. "Please, Matt, it's my fault. I need to make sure you're all right." She squeezed her eyes shut.

"Hey, sis, stop beating yourself up." Matt reached

out for her hand. "It could have happened to anyone. The bastard got me from behind. I never even saw him. I'm just sorry I let you down. And then you saved me."

Emma sniffed. "You didn't let me down." Despite her best efforts, she started crying. "I was so scared they were going to hurt you."

Donovan put his arm around her and pulled her in close. The curtain opened again, and a slim blonde-haired nurse came in. "Hi, I'm Madeline. I've got a room arranged for you, Mr. Rutledge." She looked at Emma. "I've also got a pair of scrubs that should fit you. You probably want to get out of those filthy clothes. The police are here and will interview you both."

"Clean clothes would be great, thanks."

"I've got a wheelchair here, Mr. Rutledge."

Matt grinned widely. "I can walk, Madeline. And please call me Matt." Emma snorted in a half laugh-cry.

"Hospital policy, Matt." She helped him into the wheelchair, then turned to Emma. "I'll close the curtain, and you can change in here." Releasing the brakes, she wheeled Matt out, closing the curtain to the cubicle behind her.

"Well, I better get changed. I hope I don't have to talk to Chief Rawlings." Emma sighed. "It's been an awful day, so I'm guessing he'll be here." She stepped out of her pants and pulled on the scrubs. She wrinkled her nose at the smell of her clothes.

"Yes, probably. Something this high profile will bring him out for sure." Donovan handed her the uniform top.

"Yes, I figured as much." She took off her blouse and drew the clean one over her head. "As ready as I'll ever be."

Donovan took her clothes and put them in a plastic hospital bag.

Emma screwed her face up in disgust. "No need for that. I don't ever want to see those clothes again."

"We should keep them in case the police want to examine them." He sealed the bag and drew her into him for a quick hug. He kissed her hair. "I'll be with you the whole time when you talk to the police. No need to worry."

Emma wrapped her arms around him and rested her face against his chest. "Hold me. Just hold me for a minute," she whispered. "I thought we were going to die. You know what the worst parts were?"

Donovan rocked her. "Hush."

She sniffed. "I thought I had gotten Matt killed. And that I would never see you again."

"But you didn't. You saved him. And yourself. You were amazing. You kept your head and got both of you out of there." He held her face between his hands. "I'm so proud of you. You can handle whatever Rawlings throws at you."

Emma laughed. "Absurd, huh? I escaped murderous thugs, and now I'm afraid to go talk to Chief Rawlings. Look at me. I'm shaking."

"It's not absurd at all. It's the adrenaline running through your system."

She kissed him. "Thank you."

"For what?"

"For just being you. For pulling out all the stops to find us."

"I'll always find you, Emma. You're very important to me."

"You're very important to me, Donovan."

"There you go. We're very important people." Emma laughed at the nonsensical statement.

"I'm ready now." She squared her shoulders and pulled back the curtain. "Let's get this over with."

They walked down the hall in the direction the nurse had pointed. A uniformed police officer sat in a chair in the waiting room. Emma and Donovan approached him, and he stood.

"Ms. Rutledge, I'm Officer Finley. I'd like to take your statement. The hospital has provided a room. If you would like to come with me?"

"Of course. This is Donovan Evans. I'd like him to sit in on the interview."

"Fine with me." Emma and Donovan followed him into a side room and took seats across from Officer Finley.

The officer opened his report notebook. "Tell me what happened, Ms. Rutledge."

Emma went through the events from start to finish.

"I'd like you to meet with our resident artist to do an Identikit. It will help to make a composite sketch of the kidnappers."

"Of course."

"I'll drive her to the station. I'd like you to follow us, as the kidnappers are still at large."

"Of course, Mr. Evans. Chief Rawlings wants us to do everything to ensure Ms. Rutledge's safety.

The automatic doors opened, and Jack and Ava rushed in.

"Emma!" Jack wrapped his arms around Emma and held her tightly.

"It's okay, Jack. Matt and I are fine."

"I'll see Matt in a minute. Donovan, what's going on?"

"I need to take Emma to give the police artist a description of the kidnappers."

"Ken is on a flight. He'll be here in a few hours to supervise the investigation. I don't want Rawlings involved in this." Jack's nostrils flared.

"Understood. I'll run interference." Donovan's jaw set with determination. *It had to be said.* "I won't leave her alone again. You have my word on it. I'm sorry I let you all down."

Jack held his hand out to Donovan. "You didn't let us down. There is no one I trust more. If you can't protect her, God help us all. No one could then." Donovan gripped Jack's hand in both of his.

"Thanks, old friend. Come on, Emma. Officer Finley, we're ready to go."

"Ava and I will go see Matt."

Chapter 38

They walked into the police station. A band squeezed around her head. Now wasn't the time for a tension headache. Donovan took her hand and rubbed it with the pad of this thumb.

"You've got this. You just need to work with the identikit officer and then we'll go home."

"Stay with me?"

"Always."

"Emma, Donovan, please come in." Mike gestured to a small room off to the side where they could get away from the cubicle farm. "Please sit down. We'll get started in just a few minutes. Chief Rawlings is here today, but Ken told him he would sit in on the interview himself. Ken's on his way in now."

"Good." Donovan pulled out a chair for Emma, then sat next to her. "At least this room has a window."

"I'll just get us some coffee while we wait for Ken."

"Can you also bring an aspirin for Emma?"

"Of course." Mike left the room, leaving the door ajar. Donovan took Emma's hand under the table. She smiled tremulously at him.

"Almost done, sweetheart."

"I know. I just want to get this over with and get back to the hospital. I don't want Matt to be alone."

He brought her hand to his mouth and kissed it.

"But Jack and Ava are with him now, so he's not alone. They'll make sure he's well taken care of. And Mike said they stationed a police officer outside his room."

Emma gulped. "Do you think there is still a threat? Even after all this?"

"I'm afraid so. We need to be on the alert until they run down everyone in this organization. Or at least until someone cuts a deal and names the other players so that you and Matt are no longer the sole threat to them."

There was a commotion in the bullpen area as several men in suits walked in. A cohort of men and women wearing navy windbreaker jackets with FBI emblazoned in yellow on the back carried cardboard boxes and trailed behind them. Ken brought up the rear. The men in suits went straight to the chief's office and disappeared inside to meet with Chief Rawlings. The officers in the FBI jackets spread out throughout the bullpen. They began searching the desks. Ken directed the Victoria City police officers to wait in another conference room.

"Huh." Donovan stood up to get a better look out the window of the conference room.

Emma's brow wrinkled. "What's going on?"

"If I didn't know better, I would say that the FBI are executing a search warrant."

A few minutes later, the men in suits led Chief Rawlings out in handcuffs.

"Well, well, well. It's a bad day for Chief Rawlings," Donovan drawled.

"What's happening?" Emma jumped up to peer over his shoulder.

"Chief Rawlings is doing the perp walk."

"What? He's been arrested?" Emma exclaimed,

eyes wide.

"Appears so. Here come Ken and Mike. We're about to find out what's going on."

Ken walked into the conference room with Mike. Ken trained his gaze on Emma.

"How are you doing, Emma?"

"I'm okay." She pointed at the bullpen. "What's going on?"

Ken shut the door to the conference room. "Please, sit down, and I'll explain. Then Mike will go over your statement about yesterday's events, and we'll ask you to work with the identikit officer so we can get a picture of the kidnappers out." He gestured to the chairs across from him. "First, let me apologize to you both, and particularly to you, Donovan. There's been a lot I haven't been able to share. I know Rawlings had you in interrogation for some time, Donovan. I'm sorry for that."

Donovan waved his hand in a dismissive gesture. "I wasn't worried about the questioning. It's just that it kept me from being with Emma. So she was kidnapped. I was tied up with a useless interview and couldn't help her." He turned his neck from side to side to ease the tension.

"I know. Again, I apologize to you both."

"Chief, tell us what's happening. We need the facts."

"I'll let Mike start out since he instigated everything."

Mike cleared his throat. "I was reviewing some dash cam video footage on a convenience store robbery. I accidentally brought up the wrong recording. All our dash cams are downloaded and stored for ninety days.

If there is a criminal proceeding, then the tape is stored for much longer. But anyway, I wanted to review some images taken when I responded to a robbery in progress. But the video I brought up was from Rawlings' police car. It showed him meeting with a couple guys at the boat launch ramp late at night. They were loading bundles onto a speedboat. There really wasn't a reasonable explanation for what I saw. I sent a copy of the video to the chief, and to the FBI."

Ken poured a glass of water from the pitcher on the table and took a sip. "I was already at Quantico for a training course. I was notified that the FBI would be initiating a criminal investigation. The video appeared to show Rawlings complicit in a drug deal. While it's not clear what was in the bundles, it certainly fit the pattern for illicit drug distribution. It was enough to raise questions."

"Unbelievable," Emma blurted.

"Is any of this related to Emma's assault and kidnapping?" Adrenaline rushed through Donovan's body. *Rawlings had deliberately wasted my time to allow the kidnappers access to Emma.*

"Unfortunately, yes, we think so." Ken shook his head slowly. "We think Miller was cooking and possibly running drugs for Rawlings. Since Emma was able to identify Miller, Rawlings was afraid he would cut a deal with the prosecutor and name him. So Miller clearly had to die. We haven't identified Miller's killer yet or found evidence tying it to Rawlings. But I'm confident that we will. One thing does puzzle me, though. Once Miller was dead, it's not clear to me why Rawlings continued to go after Emma."

"And who are the other men in the video? Were

you able to identify them?"

"No, it was dark, and their faces were obscured."

"So it's possible someone else thinks Emma's a threat to them or to their drug business?" Donovan asked pointedly.

Ken grimaced. "Yes. There could definitely still be a threat."

Emma's eyes watered. "I was so hoping this was over."

Donovan pulled her in close. "Hey now. We'll get there." He looked at Ken over Emma's head. Donovan's nostrils flared. "You need to get your house in order, Ken."

Ken leaned back against the chair. "Agreed."

"How deep in the department is the corruption?"

"The FBI checked into the financials of everyone at the police station. An audit showed that Rawlings is living well above his means. Officers Bartholomew and Jacoby are as well. The FBI followed the money from Rawlings to both men. They think Bartholomew and Jacoby distributed the drugs for Rawlings. So we believe they are involved. But they don't look like either man in the video. The feds are arresting them as we speak. But they're still looking at the entire department. Presumably even me, although they haven't said so."

"So, in short, the FBI don't know how deep the corruption goes, do they?"

"That's probably an accurate assessment." Ken sucked in his cheeks as if swallowing something very sour.

"All right. Now we know where we stand, even if it's not in a great place. We need to get the descriptions of the kidnappers out to the public. Emma needs to get home. This has been a traumatic day for her."

"Absolutely." Ken turned to Mike. "I'll leave this with you, Mike. I've got to go give some sort of explanation to the troops." Ken squared his shoulders as if to fortify himself.

"Will do, Chief."

Ken nodded to Donovan and Emma and left the room.

Mike picked up the desk phone and dialed an extension. "We're ready for you now." A minute later, a young woman in plain clothes and carrying a laptop entered the room. "I'm Janice. I'll be working with you on the identikit." She sat next to Emma, booted up her computer, and opened a program. "The program will ask you questions step by step, and we'll be able to build a likeness of your captors. Are you ready?"

Emma nodded. "I want to get this over with." An hour later Emma sat back in her chair and let out a huge sigh. "I'm glad that's over. Those pictures are dead ringers for the kidnappers."

"Good." Janice shut down the program. "I'm going to get these sketches out to all the officers." She left the room, closing the door behind her.

"You did great, Emma. I'm going to follow up. I'll keep you posted. But now I've got to get over to the hospital to take Matt's statement." Mike pushed back his chair and stood up

Emma looked away for a minute, then back to Mike. She swallowed deeply.

"Do you think you'll find them?"

Mike cleared his throat. "I'll be completely honest with you, Emma. I can't promise we'll find them, but I can promise the chief and I will do everything possible to hunt them down and bring them to justice."

"That's not exactly what I wanted to hear." Emotion choked her voice. "But I guess that's all I can ask."

Mike turned to Donovan. "I'll be in touch as soon as I have any more information."

Donovan nodded. He put his hand on the small of Emma's back. "Let's go home."

Chapter 39

Donovan stood in Jack's office, looking out the picture window.

Jack walked over to the wall cabinet, opened a lower door, and took out a bottle of whiskey. He held it up to Donovan.

"Join me?"

Donovan looked over his shoulder and eyed the expensive brand of liquor.

"Yeah, thanks."

Jack poured a measure into two glasses and handed one to his friend. "Other than my sister's assault and kidnapping, what's bothering you?"

"What makes you think something is troubling me?"

Jack snorted. "How long have we been friends?"

"Long enough."

"Right. Sufficient time for me to know when you are worried. Spill it before the ladies join us."

Donovan swirled the whiskey in his glass. "I'm not sure what's disturbing me. Something just doesn't add up."

"Like what?"

"I can't put my finger on it. Just a feeling." He paused, frowning, and took a swallow of the whiskey. He stared intently into his glass. "Rawlings doesn't strike me as a drug kingpin. That guy couldn't put a deal together if his life depended on it. So how did he assemble a team to distribute the drugs? And where did he get the people to cook the meth? And organize the locations? As much as I hate to admit this, being the head of a drug cartel takes organizational and leadership skills. I just don't see Rawlings as a criminal mastermind."

Jack raised an eyebrow. "Well, maybe he isn't. That's why he got caught."

"Hmm...No, I don't think so. There's someone else who is pulling the strings here. Someone else is giving the orders. Rawlings is just a fall guy."

"So maybe Rawlings will cut a deal with prosecutors and flip on the real drug lord."

Donovan shook his head. "Experience tells us he won't live that long. Miller was killed pretty quickly. Rawlings is a dead man walking."

"So how do we figure out who the real crime boss is?"

"That's the problem, isn't it? And Emma won't be safe until the head of the operation is in custody." Donovan stared morosely into his glass.

There was a knock on the door, and Ava poked her head in.

"Matt called. They're discharging him from the hospital. Mike is going to drive him over here. We should have him stay with us for a few days until he recovers fully."

"Absolutely." Jack held up his half-empty glass. "We'll be out in just a minute."

Ava nodded and shut the study door.

"You'll have a full house. Are you sure you want Emma and me to stay here as well?"

Jack looked at him intently. "I wouldn't have it any other way. Family first, man. Always."

"Thanks, Jack."

Jack narrowed his eyes. "On that note, how are things progressing with Emma? Are you going to make an honest woman of her?"

Donovan exploded in a laugh. "I'm damn sure trying. In between trying to keep her safe from assorted criminals."

"Good. I look forward to the day you are actually my brother."

"Yeah, me too."

Chapter 40

"I've got another viewing scheduled today for Ed."
Emma slathered peanut butter on her whole wheat toast
and looked around the table, trying to gauge the
reactions. Jack, Ava, Matt, and Donovan were all
finishing up the breakfast that Elsa had made. Things
were getting back to normal.

Donovan crossed his arms over his chest. "I'm not
sure that's a good idea. I'm not convinced that the FBI
have this all wrapped up."

"I know. But how long will it take them to
complete their investigation? It could be
weeks…months…Heck, it could even be years. I can't
put my job on hold."

"It's not my decision, but for what it's worth, I
agree with Donovan," Jack interjected. "The company
can front you a salary if you're worried about losing
commissions."

"Thanks, Jack. But I need to get back to work."
Emma's voice cracked.

"I'll go with you. And we'll screen your clients
very carefully. Anyone who doesn't have a cast iron
alibi for the last seven years of their life won't be taken
on as a client."

Emma rolled her eyes at Donovan's commanding
tone. "Fine. I'm not unreasonable. I don't want anyone
else to get hurt like Matt did. In fact, until this settles

down, I think all our agents should have some additional protocols. Maybe going in pairs and checking in by phone regularly with the office when they are out showing homes."

"That sounds like a good policy to institute. Meanwhile, Donovan can go with you."

"All right." Emma nodded, conceding the point to them. She turned to Donovan. "Ed's found a home by word of mouth. I'm glad. He was disappointed when his offer wasn't accepted. He'd like to see it at three today. Does that work for you, Donovan?"

"Sure. I'll make myself available any time you need me."

Emma forced the reasons for the new procedures to the back of her mind. She turned to Ava. "How is your father's recovery coming along?"

Ava blinked rapidly and gave a shaky smile. "He's doing well, thanks, Emma. He needs to watch his diet and exercise. But on the positive side, he's talking about scaling back his law practice. Maybe even retiring. That means they can spend more time at their condo here."

"That's wonderful, Ava."

Ava glanced at Jack who nodded imperceptibly.

"My mom's delighted on so many levels. She's wanted my father to retire for several years now. And if they spend more time at their condo, they'll be able to see their grandchild more often."

Emma jumped out of her chair. She ran around the table to hug Ava. "Does that mean what I think it means? Are you pregnant?"

"It does. I am." Ava broke out into a wide grin. "It's been so difficult not to say anything."

A cacophony of voices erupted.

"Congratulations!"

"Wonderful news!"

Elsa came in to clear the plates, beaming. "I can't wait to have a little one in the house."

Ava reached over and held Jack's hand.

"It was a little earlier than we planned, but we can't wait." Jack squeezed Ava's hand gently.

Chapter 41

Emma turned into the driveway of the colonial style house. Donovan looked at the well-kept house and yard. "It doesn't have water access. Isn't that important to Ed?"

"It was. But he insisted that he wanted to see this house. You know how it goes. The client is always right. And half the time, they end up buying something completely different than what they say they want." She shrugged.

A white truck pulled into the driveway. "There's Ed now. Let's see how this goes."

Ed parked his truck next to her SUV and got out of his vehicle. "Hi, Emma. Thanks for making time to see this property with me."

"It's no trouble. And besides, you're my hero." Emma kissed Ed on the cheek. Ed looked down and shuffled his feet.

"I was surprised that you wanted to see this house, Ed. It doesn't have water access."

"Yes, w-well, I've been doing a lot of thinking. My wife might be right. I spend too much time fishing. My buddy told me about this house. It might appeal to my wife."

Emma tried to keep her face blank. Ed chuckled.

"I can see from the look on your face that you're wondering whether I'm deluding myself. I understand.

But Debbie and I have been going to counseling at the High Road Church. She thinks she might give me another chance."

"Ed, that's wonderful news. But do you want to give up something you love? You would be changing for the sake of your marriage."

"Debbie's not asking me to give up fishing all together. She's just asking me to limit it to twice a month. I can see now that I've been neglecting her when I was out fishing all the time."

Emma beamed at him. "That's wonderful news indeed. But if that is the case, shouldn't Debbie be here to view the house with you?"

Ed's face turned red, and he shuffled his feet. "I wanted to have a look first. I didn't want her falling in love with a place that I couldn't stand."

"Very sensible. Let's go in and take a look." Emma unlocked the lock box and retrieved the key. "Did your friend say when this is coming to market?"

Ed shook his head. "They're in the process of cleaning out some of their stuff."

"Okay. That's fine. Keep in mind that most sellers will want to test the market. I doubt they will be open to a low initial offer until it's been on the market a while."

"I understand."

They passed through the entryway into a great room. The corners of Ed's mouth turned up.

"This room would be great for my football parties. Look at that space for a large screen television."

"Wonderful. Let's check out the kitchen, and you can see if Debbie might like it." Emma guided him into the kitchen/dining area. Donovan trailed behind them.

Ed looked around. "She would love this kitchen.

She's always wanted a granite island. She needs the room for all her baking."

Emma suppressed a smile "There are additional rooms downstairs. A study and guest room. There is also a half bathroom."

Ed wandered in the direction of the study.

Emma looked at Donovan. "This doesn't meet his stated requirements, but he seems to love it."

"I guess you just can't tell."

"I know. It's always that way. You can never predict what a client will like."

"Come on. Let's go find Ed and make sure he hasn't gotten lost. He's pretty quiet."

Emma led the way to the study. She opened the door. "Ed, what do you think?" She stopped. Ed was as white and still as a marble statute with sweat beading on his forehead. Realtor Pete Magnuson pointed a gun at Ed's head.

"Pete? What's going on? What are you doing?"

"Freaking Emma. You've been a real pain in the ass. I should never have sent others to do my work. Don't move, or I'll put a bullet in his head."

"We're not moving. There is no need to harm anyone." Donovan held his hands up and kept his voice calm.

"You brought the boyfriend, Emma? That's kind of amateurish, don't you think?"

A hysterical gurgle burst out of Emma. "Don't you think holding a gun on someone is unprofessional?"

"Well now, I guess it depends on the business, doesn't it?" Pete smirked.

"And a gun is standard in the drug trade, isn't it Pete?" Donovan stated. "Weren't you making enough money selling houses?"

Emma gulped. *Is Donovan really making small talk with a man holding a gun?*

Donovan kept his focus on Pete.

"I made some bad investments. Got hit by negative equity in the last housing market crash." His face contorted. "What was I to do? I needed to make some money fast."

"So you started running drugs?" Emma squeezed her eyes shut.

"You Rutledges are so high and mighty. The great Jack Rutledge wouldn't sully his hands in a shady deal." A vein on the side of Pete's neck throbbed.

"That's right. He wouldn't." Out of the corner of her eye, she saw Donovan nod encouragingly to her. *He wants me to distract Pete.* "Stop, Pete! You don't have to do this. We can arrange for some other investors to help you with your projects. We'll find a way out for you." *You deserve to rot in jail.* Emma hoped her real thoughts weren't showing.

Pete's face twisted into an ugly mask. His arm shook with adrenaline-fueled rage. "It's too late. You don't understand. I need to supply the drugs to my distributor. I know too much. If I talk, I'm a dead man."

"So you've been cooking meth? Do you know how many people that kills?" Emma's voice shook.

"They have miserable lives anyway." Pete's tone was dismissive. He gestured with the gun, and it wavered temporarily away from Ed's head.

Donovan hurled himself at Pete, tackling him and knocking his gun arm down. Pete's hand tightened, and he pulled the trigger. The bullet whizzed past Ed and lodged in the wall. Donovan hit the ground, with Pete on the bottom, breaking his fall. "You bastard. You're lucky I don't kill you." He yanked Pete's hands behind his back.

"Get the gun, Emma."

Emma hurried over and picked up the gun. Donovan looked up at Ed.

"You okay?"

Ed's chin bobbed. "Thanks."

"Give me your belt."

Ed froze for a few seconds with his hands on the webbed belt on his pants.

"Oh, right." He shook himself out of his stupor and pulled it off and handed it to Donovan. Donovan secured Pete's hands behind his back.

"Ed, can you handle a gun?"

"I grew up hunting."

"Emma, give him the gun. Ed, if he moves, shoot him."

Ed took the gun and held it with an easy grip. "I may shoot him even if he doesn't move."

"Emma, stay here and call 911. Then call Mike. I'm going to check out the rest of the house to see if he has any friends."

"Be careful, Donovan," Emma whispered.

"I will." Donovan shut the door behind him. Emma pulled her phone out to call the police. Donovan came back in just a few minutes.

"The house is empty. I don't see any other cars, but I assume Pete parked a few streets away. Let's get to a more defensible position in case he has friends coming. How long until the police get here?"

"About ten minutes. Same for Mike too."

"I want you to stay away from windows. Emma,

get behind the desk. Ed, do the same, but make sure you have a clean line of sight to fire on Pete."

Emma crawled behind the desk. Ed followed but kept to the side where he still had a clear shot.

Donovan positioned himself to the side of the window, so he would be able to see anyone who came through the study door.

"You've got to let me go." Pete's shoulders slumped. "I'll forget your involvement."

"Shut up, Pete, before I kill you because you hurt Emma," Donovan snarled.

"She was just collateral damage." Pete squirmed on the floor. "You understand that. These things happen."

Ed leaned away from the desk and kicked him. "Take that you asshole."

Sirens wailed in the background.

"Thank goodness." Emma's voice shook with relief. Her cell phone rang, and she glanced at the screen. "It's Mike."

"Throw it to me," Donovan ordered.

Emma tossed her mobile to him.

Donovan hit the answer button. "We're in the study downstairs. We have control of the situation. Ed has a gun on Pete Magnuson who threatened us. No one else is in the house. Don't shoot us."

"Acknowledged. I'll let the uniforms know."

A door creaked, and the thud of heavy feet scattered throughout the house. Loud voices headed their way. The door burst open, and two police officers in bullet proof vests and helmets rushed into the room. Mike followed behind them. Ed crouched and set the gun on the floor. He kicked it over to one of the police officers. The other officer handcuffed Pete and pulled him to his feet.

Mike looked at Pete and shook his head. "Well, well, well. Pete Magnuson. As I recall from high school, you were voted most likely to screw up. I guess they were right."

Pete glared at him.

"Read him his rights and arrest him for assault with a deadly weapon and distribution of controlled substances. No doubt we'll be adding more charges."

The officer grabbed Pete. "Come on, Pete. You sold my elderly aunt a dump of a house. For that alone, I hope they throw the book at you. You have the right to remain silent." He opened the front door and helped Pete down the front steps. "Anything you say…"

Mike raised an eyebrow. "You just can't keep out of trouble, can you?"

"It appears not." Donovan raised his hands in a "what can you do" gesture.

Ed cleared his throat. "I know you need a statement, but can I look at the rest of the house first? I reckon my wife would like this place."

They all laughed. Mike gestured to Ed and Emma. "Feel free to look upstairs, but don't take too long."

"Come on, Ed. Let's go." She and Ed left the room and headed to the second floor just as Ken walked into the study.

"Well done. You wrapped up the drug trade locally, Donovan."

"I think we are finally there, Chief."

"Federal agents are at the station. They're going to process Magnuson on federal charges. That should keep him locked up a good long time. The FBI have scattered their net wide. They hope to pick up Mindy and her coconspirators soon."

"Just as long as he doesn't go to Club Fed."

"Not a chance. He and Rawlings can conspire together all they want in jail, but their prison experience won't be pleasant."

"Just one more question, Chief."

"Go ahead."

"Was the High Road Church involved at all?"

"To the best of my knowledge, no. They appear to be just a bunch of slightly naïve but well intentioned 'do gooders.' They really thought they could help Robert Miller. As often as I say there are no coincidences, this appears to be one."

Chapter 42

Emma opened the door to the Salon by the Sea. It was a high concept salon decorated in shades of blue. Glamorous photographs of women with elegant hair styles hung on the walls. A bookshelf displayed expensive hair products for sale. The side wall had a mural of a beach scene. Several customers flipped through magazines while they waited for their stylist. Emma waved to Nancy, one of the hair stylists, who was blow drying a client's hair.

"Hi, Emma. Good to see you. If you're here to see Ann-Marie, she's finished for the day. She's in the back working on some paperwork. She should be just about done. She's been back there about an hour."

"Thanks, Nancy. I'll see if she's free." She headed toward the back of the salon and knocked on the office door.

"Come on in."

Emma opened the door and peered in. "Are you ready for a break? I've brought your favorite latte." She held up cups of take-out coffee.

Ann-Marie looked up from the old-fashioned ledger. "You're a life saver! I'd love one. And a break would be great. These numbers are all running together." She rubbed her face wearily.

Emma handed her the hot drink and pulled up a chair. Ann-Marie inhaled the fragrant steam from the caramel-flavored treat. She took a sip and sighed. "Pure heaven."

Emma laughed. "I know. It's the simple things in life, huh?"

"You said it. It's good to see you happy again. You've been through some rough times lately."

Emma let out a huge exhalation of pent-up breath. "I can't believe it's finally over. It seems like a bad dream that I just want to forget. Then I wake up and see Donovan. And it was all worth it."

"Girl, you got a good one there. He's a keeper. And he's so hot." Ann-Marie used her hand to fan herself. She paused. "I'm glad you finally opened up and took the risk to trust someone. We both have issues. I'm glad one of us has gotten past it." She gave a wan smile. "I'm very happy for you, Emma."

"Thanks, Ann-Marie. I know. He's pretty great. Who am I kidding? He's amazing." Emma's lips parted in a silly grin. "Sometimes I have to pinch myself. On another note, I feel like I've neglected you lately. I'm sorry I had to cancel our spa day. What do you think about rescheduling it? Checking ourselves in for some treatments and relaxation?"

"That sounds wonderful. When were you thinking?"

"How about Monday? Your salon is closed, but the hotel spa will still be open."

"Perfect."

"That's great. I'll make reservations. How late are you working tonight? Do you want to come by for dinner?"

Ann-Marie grimaced. "I'd love to. But I need to work on these accounts. I can't get the damn numbers to work."

"Anything I can do to help? Or I'm sure Ava would help. In fact, she's taking on some small clients in addition to being the Chief Financial Officer at Rutledge Properties."

"Thanks, Emma. I don't think it's anything Ava could help with. The problem is pretty simple. I need to get income up and expenses down. The landlord raised our rent—no offense—and I don't have any room to add another hairstylist station to generate more revenue."

Concern flickered in her eyes. "I didn't realize you were having problems. I know Jack raised the rent. He did a review of the rental rates of all the commercial buildings and adjusted them to keep up with inflation."

A look of sadness crossed her face. "It's not something I'm comfortable talking about."

"I don't mean to pry, but I'm worried about you. We're friends. We care about each other. We help each other." Emma reached out to put her hand on Ann-Marie's arm. "Have you discussed this with your silent partner? Maybe come up with some ideas to diversify and get some more income streams into the salon?"

Ann-Marie's gaze drifted to the wall, then the door, anywhere but at Emma.

"What's wrong?" Emma's senses pinged on high alert.

"Nothing, Emma." She glanced at her but broke eye contact.

"Come on. We've shared a lot since you opened your salon five years ago. I've seen you pull yourself together after Joe left with all your savings. We've always been honest and open with each other."

"My silent partner is no longer part of the business," Ann-Marie said quietly and fiddled with her coffee cup.

"What happened? I thought you had a great arrangement. He was free with the cash but never around to tell you how to spend it. You were so lucky to get an influx of capital to open the salon." Emma paused. Her heart skipped a beat. Ann-Marie looked down at her desk.

"No!" The word burst out of her. "Tell me what I'm thinking isn't true." Her voice dropped. "Please."

Ann-Marie refused to look at her.

Bile rose up her throat. *It couldn't be, could it?* Emma spoke slowly, her voice flat. "It's Pete, isn't it? Who else but a drug dealer has a ready supply of easy money? That's why he's no longer your silent partner? Because he's in jail?" Anger poured through her veins while she waited for Ann-Marie's response. She shook with rage.

Ann-Marie fiddled with a pencil. Finally, she put the pencil down.

"When Pete first invested, did you know the money was dirty?"

Ann-Marie cleared her throat. "I didn't know for sure."

A fresh wave of fury consumed her. "But you suspected?"

Her reply was barely audible. "Yes."

"How could you?" Emma bit out the words. "You knew all along that Pete was dirty. You knew drug dealers were after me." Her voice grew high and shrill. "You should have come forward and told the police about Pete. You should have told me."

Ann-Marie slammed her accounts book closed. "You don't understand. You don't have to worry about paying the rent for the salon. Or for my apartment. Joe left me shortly after we moved here, and that bastard took all of my savings. I had to get the salon open, and I no longer had the funds. I needed to keep a roof over my head. I needed to eat. And I had no safety net. Pete needed a business to invest in."

Emma reeled back, a hand to her chest. "To invest in? Or to launder his drug money?"

Ann-Marie quivered with anger. "Don't take the high road with me. Your moneybags brother would never let you worry about paying your bills."

Emma blinked twice. "He tried to kill me. Several times. And you never said anything. You never said anything. You would have let him kill me to protect your business." She put her coffee down on the desk, stood, and left the office, closing the door quietly behind her.

Chapter 43

Donovan switched on the steamer. Thick clouds billowed, and he ran it along the wallpaper in the bathroom in the owner's suite. The wallpaper loosened, and he peeled off a strip. He ran the steamer down the wall again and pulled off some more. He got into a rhythm and made steady progress. The hinges of the front door creaked, and a minute later Emma appeared in the doorway.

"I've brought lunch." She held up a basket and showed him the containers of food. "Are you ready for a break?"

Donovan looked at the wallpaper steamer which had taken a long time to come up to temperature and then back at Emma. He had a fair amount more to do, but it was an easy decision.

"Of course. I'm definitely ready for a break." He set the tool down.

He fingered the jeweler's ring box in his pocket. He'd been carrying it around with him for weeks, waiting for the right time.

He gestured to the basket. "What's for lunch?"

Emma pulled back the towel covering the contents. "Elsa packed a choice of chicken salad sandwiches or her island-famous homemade pimiento cheese sandwiches. There's also some of her pasta salad, and fresh baked apple pie for dessert. We could have a picnic on the patio."

Donovan's eyes glinted with pleasure. "That sounds like a perfect idea. Just give me a few minutes to get cleaned up." He gestured to the white coveralls he wore over a T-shirt and shorts.

"I'll just set things up outside. Take your time." Emma wandered out into the living room, and then out onto the patio. Donovan turned on the shower. He stripped out of the coveralls, then his clothes, and stepped under the water. The cold water hitting him was a shock. He quickly washed away the dust created by the renovation before turning off the water. He toweled dry, dressed in a clean pair of shorts and T-shirt, and put the ring back in his pocket. He found Emma on the patio, setting out the food on a blanket.

She waved her hand expansively. "Picture your plunge pool here, with some patio seating over there. With the view of the ocean, this will be perfect."

"It is perfect." Donovan looked directly at her and not the ocean.

Emma's face heated. She turned away and fiddled with the containers, setting out the food.

Donovan blew out a breath. *Enough. This has to stop. My patience has come to an end.* "Emma. Do I make you uncomfortable?"

Emma looked up at him. "No, of course not." She lowered her gaze to the picnic basket.

He sighed in frustration. "I've been giving you space, but I'm starting to think that was the wrong strategy. Talk to me, Emma."

She hesitated. *I owe him an explanation.* "I know I've been a bit distant lately, well, since Pete's arrest. I'm sorry for that."

He took both her hands in his. "Let me help you, Emma. You've been through a lot of traumatic events."

She stared out to the ocean. "I've just, well, I've just been questioning all my decisions. Someone I knew for years tried to kill me. And my best friend knew and didn't do anything. How could I have missed that?" Her voice shook. "I guess—I guess I just needed a little time and space to process everything that happened. Ann-Marie's betrayal hit me hard. We were friends for over five years." Her voice broke. "Even Pete's actions felt personal. We worked in the same circles for years. We saw each other at all the major social functions. It's a small island. Everyone knows everyone."

Donovan pulled her into a hug and rubbed her back.

"It's not easy to accept that someone you knew wanted to kill you. And worse, a close friend suspected and said nothing," she continued in a monotone. "She would have let me be killed rather than cut off the money supply for her salon."

He rocked her gently. "I know it's hard, kitten. Dishonesty from someone close is never easy. Everyone missed it. Not just you. Pete presented a normal face to the world. There was no way you could have known that he was behind a drug ring." Donovan took her chin and tilted her face so she looked at him. "I know it hurts. You're not the first person to be deceived by someone you know and trust, and you won't be the last. It is hard to come to terms with. But you can't let it rule your life. Ann-Marie was weak. She took Pete's dirty money and couldn't get out. I'll never forgive her for not telling the police that it was likely Pete who was after you. But karma is a bitch. She's lost her salon after Jack canceled her lease on the building. She became a social pariah and has had to leave the island. She's ruined here. And she may still face criminal charges for her involvement. Pete was an acquaintance, and you were friendly. But you never got closer than that. On some level, you knew he wasn't someone you wanted to be friends with. My grandfather used to say that you could count the people you could trust on one hand. The rest were just contacts. I've always found that to be true. Think about who you have faith in."

Her face softened as tension drained away. "I believe in you."

He ran his finger down the side of her face and kissed her gently. "I'm glad. I have faith in you." He pulled back from the kiss and looked at her. "In fact, I love you. I always have, even if I didn't let myself near you."

Her eyes watered. *So long. I have waited so long for you, Donovan. It's hard to believe the moment has come.* "I love you, too."

"Good." He pulled the ring box out of the pocket of his shorts and opened it. A diamond solitaire set in platinum glinted in the sun. "Emma, will you marry me?"

She gasped. "Oh Donovan, it's beautiful." Tears ran down her face. "Yes. Yes. Yes."

Laughing, he wiped away her tears and pressed a gentle kiss on her mouth. "Come on. Let's have lunch and then go share the news with your family."

She reached up to kiss him. "I love it when you're right. Although don't expect me to admit that again."

Epilogue

*Six months later*

"Donovan, do you have the ice bucket?" She held up a bottle of champagne.

Donovan opened the door from the patio. A black Labrador puppy ran between his legs. He leaned down and gave Emma a kiss. "I've got it right here, sweetheart. And I've got more bottles in the wine chiller."

"Good. Thanks." She looked around with a critical eye and fluffed a sofa pillow.

He sighed. "Everything is perfect. We're ready for this party. Don't worry." He scooped up the wriggling dog. "I've been hoping Ares would run some energy off before the party."

Emma scoffed. "Not much chance of that." She leaned in, and Ares licked her face. "I just want everything to be just right. This is our big reveal."

Donovan laughed. "Everyone has pretty much been here at some point during the renovations. I don't think there are any surprises."

He set the squirming puppy down and pulled her into his arms. Emma relaxed as she leaned into his embrace. "I guess I'm being a bit silly, aren't I?"

"Just a bit. But I love that about you." He kissed the top of her head.

Emma laughed. "Good thing you qualified that statement."

"Now that the remodeling is done, we should think about our next party."

"Yeah? What's that?" She looked at him quizzically.

"Our wedding. There are no more reasons to put it off. We don't need to manage the contractors, so there will be time to plan the wedding. Ava and Jack have had their baby, so Ava's objection to being in the wedding party is moot. And before you say it, we are not waiting until Maddie is old enough to be a flower girl."

Emma bust out laughing. "I wasn't planning to wait until Maddie could be in the wedding party. In fact, I agree. It's time. I can't wait to be Mrs. Evans."

"Good. That's settled then. We'll pick a date and get started planning."

"You know what?"

"What is it, sweetheart?"

"Let's get married on the beach. A small wedding. Just immediate family. What do you think?"

"If that means we get married sooner, then I'm all for it. That keeps it simple. We won't have to worry about who we need to invite."

"Yeah, that could be tricky. As an elected official, you can't afford to alienate people. This way, it won't matter because only family will be invited."

His smile slipped. "You don't mind that I decided to run for the bench instead of working for Jack, do you?"

"You've made a wonderful judge. Wise and fair. I'm happy that you enjoy what you are doing and are doing it well. The community needs good people like you. I couldn't be more delighted with the way things turned out."

He pressed his lips to hers gently then leaned his forehead against hers. "Me too."

The doorbell rang.

"Come on, almost Mrs. Evans." He held his hand out to her. "Let's start the rest of our lives."

## A word about the author...

Karen Andover is an author of romantic suspense and contemporary romance. Karen lives an idyllic island life and her goal is to share her happy place with readers one book at a time. She lives in Florida with her husband and rescue pup. www.karenandover.com